Enid Blyton

KT-547-597

THE diary of the NAUGHTiEST GiRL

Hodder Children's Books

Reimagined by

Jeanne Willis

Illustrations by Alex T. Smith

3 5 7 9 10 8 6 4

A CIP catalogue record for this book is available from the British Library.

ISBN 978-1-444-93257-7

Typeset in Old Claude LP by Avon DataSet Ltd, Bidford-on-Avon, Warwickshire
Printed and bound in Great Britain by Clays Lyd, St Ives plc

The paper and board used in this book are made from wood
from responsible sources

Hodder Children's Books
An imprint of Hachette Children's Group
Part of Hodder and Stoughton
Carmelite House, 50 Victoria Embankment, London, EC4Y 0DZ

An Hachette UK Company
www.hachette.co.uk

SATURDAY

Dear Diary,

Actually, no! You are not a *Dear Diary* at all. I hate you. You are pink and thick and spotty like my cousin Nelly. I am so angry I could rip you to bits . . . Why? Because when Mum said she had the perfect gift for me if I stopped sulking, guess what? I thought you were a new laptop to say how sorry she is that she's skulking off with Daddy to study baboons in Africa for months on end . . . without me!

Yes, you heard – without ME!

Seriously, what kind of terrible parents abandon their only child for baboons and don't even buy her a laptop,

1

a pony or a teacup piglet to make up for it? And new trainers, obviously.

Not much to ask, is it? I mentioned this in a perfectly calm way to Mum but all she said was, 'Don't shout, Elizabeth. It's a lovely diary – it's faux ostrich leather. You can fill it with all the fun things you'll do at the wonderful boarding school we're sending you to.'

So I said v politely, 'Ostrich? I don't care if it's made from unicorn leather. It's gross, it hasn't got a plug and it won't be "fun" or "wonderful" at Whyteleafe School because I'm NOT going!'

Then I might have stamped my feet slightly and threatened to call ChildLine but I never said the rude word she *thought* I said. I don't know why Mum sent me to my room. Before I slammed the door, I pointed out v gently that she is bound to have hearing loss now that she's thirty-six and that she'd totally misheard me but she simply replied, 'I think Whyteleafe School will do us both the world of good, darling,' and walked off. So rude.

Well, I'm NOT going to that awful school – I shan't!

I'm going to stay right here with my guinea pigs and my pony and Kesi can try to look after me till my parents come back – *if* they ever come back. They might get eaten by crocodiles if I'm not around to keep an eye on them and then they'll be sorry. I feel sooo UNWANTED! Do you know how it feels not to be wanted, Diary? OK, I'll show you.

Now, either you find your own way to the wheelie bin or I will:

A) Flush you down the toilet

B) Feed you to my guinea pigs

C) All I'm saying is, I know where Kesi hides the matches . . .

4

Dear Diary,

Sorry I tried to set fire to you. Love you really. It's not your fault you're not a laptop. When I'm upset, I take my feelings out on everything and everyone but I don't mean to. Bet that's why Mum and Dad aren't taking me to Africa. They said it's because 'it's a work trip not a holiday'. Yeah right. I know Daddy has to go because he's a top monkey professor – what I *don't* get is why Mum has to tag along, taking photos of baboons' bums, when she should be staying at home to give me lifts to Pony Club. So selfish.

You're lucky not to have feelings, Diary. You've got a tiny singe on your cover but it'll rub off and I saved you by smothering you in the Persian rug, didn't I? I'm surprised it set off the smoke alarm – there was only a bit of smouldering – but Kesi completely overreacted and called the fire brigade. Told her there was no need, and I could tell the chief firefighter was on my side. He got quite narky with Kesi for dialling 999 and wasting his time and the tax payers' money over a false alarm.

The firefighters have gone now. Kesi is on the warpath again, so I am hiding in the broom cupboard. She's mad at me because I found her matches. For some stupid reason I'm not allowed to have them after what happened last time. All I did was use one tiny match to heat some crystals from my chemistry set after my private science tutor walked out on me, like all the others. How was I to know that the test tube would explode?

It didn't do nearly as much damage as everyone said. The hole in the bathroom ceiling wasn't that big and it wasn't like whole toilet seat melted – only the lid. Thought M & D would be glad I'd done my science project, but there's no pleasing them.

PANTS! They're back from the shops. Mum will freak out when she sees the rug. It's just a bit of soot on a few tassels but she's ridiculously house-proud. I'd blame it on my little brother but she never gave me one because she's too busy bothering baboons.

SUNDAY

Dear Diary,

I am NOT crying. I'm just washing my eyes with tears.

Still washing them.

All right, I'm crying. Things are going from bad to worse. Sorry to make your pages damp. I'll be OK in a minute. Will just blow my nose on the duvet and then tell you what happened.

Ready for this?

My pocket money has been stopped for a whole week, even though I showed great initiative in preventing a fire.

My phone has also been confiscated. When I said I needed it for boarding school (even though I am not going), Mum said pupils aren't allowed to take mobile devices to Whyteleafe to:

- Prevent misuse
- Promote independence
- Encourage letter-writing and the art of conversation
- Pursue healthy outdoor activities

Excuse me? It's the twenty-first century! What next? Ride to school on a penny-farthing? Do my homework on papyrus with a stick? Wear a whalebone corset and a crinoline for PE?

Cousin Nelly gets to foster my guinea pigs, Sausage & Beans, when M & D are away. Hope they poop in her stupid bobble hat.

Ross is going to be stabled at the farm and ridden by Christabel Cardew, the snobbiest girl ever. Imagine a moose in jodhpurs – that's her. I don't want her riding Ross. He'll sag in the middle when she mounts him. Hope he tosses her in a hedge.

But this is nothing – *NOTHING* – compared to what Mum said next.

When I told her Whyteleafe isn't happening and that I'm staying RIGHT here with Kesi and my animals – shock horror! She broke the dreadful news that she's been keeping from me, which is this:

Kesi is going away. For ever. Without ME! Why, why, why? She has looked after me since I was born in Kenya, the first time M & D went over there to do monkey business. Afterwards, she came to England to live with us because she loved me so much. Why doesn't she love me any more? I'm not that bad, am I?

Things I've Done to Kesi That Made Her Laugh:

- Put a rubber snake in her bed
- Cut the left cup out of her bra to make an Easter bonnet

- Borrowed her wig to style my snowman

I think she was laughing. Mum said it was hysteria but how does she know? She's a journalist, not a doctor. I won't let Kesi go. I won't! When she comes into my room to help me pack for Tightebriefe School, to which I'm NOT going, I will:

1. Tip everything out of my suitcase.
2. Fling my arms round Kesi + promise to be good.
3. Beg her to stay.
4. Tie her to a chair with my skipping rope if she tries to escape.

Wish me luck. This is E. Allen signing off till I get my own way.

M⊙NDAY

Dear Diary,

I'm back. Sorry to report that Kesi has escaped.
What she doesn't know is that she's just walked to
Tesco wearing a tail. HA, HA, HAAAAA!

It's her fault for deserting me. I asked her how
she could be going away to look after her new
grandchild when I need looking after and she said,
'You're eleven years old. Time you grew up, young
lady.' Then she started banging on about all the
things she had to do when *she* was eleven, like:

- Look after ten brothers + sisters
- Milk chickens
- Collect goat eggs
- Wash clothes in a crocodile-infested river
- All without moaning

Then Kesi started packing the hideous tights I'm supposed to wear at Spiteleafe even though I'm NOT going. So I said, 'I *hate* tights! They always fall down + make me walk like I've wet myself. I'm a *sock* girl.'

And Kesi said, 'You are a *spoilt* girl. Not everyone is lucky enough to have an education. You should be grateful for a smart uniform and nice new tights and wear them with pride.'

Am not grateful! The Tighteleafe uniform is gross. I won't be seen dead in it. It's got a kilt and a beret. Who do they think I am, a Scottish onion seller? I am *not* wearing a beret. It looks like a cowpat. If they make me wear it, I will stamp on it and throw it up a tree.

Oh, and if Kesi thinks my tights are so nice, *she* can wear them, which is why I pinned them on her skirt

13

like a tail. Did it without her noticing when she fished my beret out of the bin after I threw it across the room like a Frisbee ... Good shot! She'll laugh about it later when she gets back from Tesco wagging her tail behind her.

Tuesday

Dear Diary,

Kesi didn't find her tail funny. It got caught in someone's trolley wheel in the cheese aisle. I laughed like a hyena when she told me but she just tutted and said the sooner she goes home, the better, like she wants to get away from me, for some reason.

I thought she was joking so I said, 'You'll miss me when I'm gone,' thinking she'd burst into tears and say, 'You're right. I can't leave you, Elizabeth.

I love you more than I love my own children. I will stay here with you + promise never to leave.'

But she didn't say any of that. She said, 'I'm tired of being the butt of your jokes, Elizabeth.'

So I said, 'The joke's on your butt, Kesi!' because of the tail thing, but instead of laughing at my hilarious quip, she went all serious, like I'd pinned the tights on to upset her. I wouldn't upset Kesi for the world. I love her to bits. I told her that but she didn't say it back like she usually does.

When I tried to cuddle her and say sorry, she said, 'The trouble with you is that people have loved you too much, Elizabeth. They fuss you + spoil you + let you wind them round your little finger.'

And when I said that's because I'm so adorable, Kesi said it isn't enough to have a pretty face (thanks) and that I need a good heart (like I haven't got one) and *then* she said something so hurtful I can't even bring myself to tell you. Too upset to write now.

Wednesday

Dear Diary,

I am so over what Kesi said yesterday. It's rubbish that I need to go to school to learn how to behave. I *know* how to behave. I just don't want to. Don't care if I haven't got any friends, I don't want to be taught with other kids – especially boys. I met a boy once and he was stupid. He was like another species. Anyway, I like having private tutors. Not my fault if six have left.

I've got a plan. I'm going to be so good for the rest of the week, M & D and Kesi won't recognise me. They'll think I've been replaced by an angel. Then they will have to change their mind about sending me to Frightleafe and they'll take me to Africa or let me to stay here. Fine. Don't care which.

Good Things I'm Going to Do to Change M and D's Minds:

- Clean out Sausage + Beans's hutch every day
- Hang clothes up + tidy bedroom
- Bring cups + plates down and put in the dishwasher
- Make own bed
- Help with hoovering
- Make M, D and K friendship bracelets
- Say please + thank you
- Be nice to Nelly

Bad Things I'm NOT Going to Do:

- Scream/swear/stamp my feet
- Ask for more pocket money
- Play practical jokes
- Slam my bedroom door
- Keep asking for stuff
- Say there's nothing in the fridge

- Laugh at Dad's clothes/hair/dancing
- Play with my mobile at the dinner table

Believe me, it will work.

THURSDAY

Dear Diary,

Well, *that* didn't work. Been so good for two whole days, I feel sick.

Nelly actually thinks I'm her new best friend.

The guinea pig hutch is so clean I ate my dinner off it.

Told Dad he looked great in jeans.

Pretended to Mum she looked slim.

Braided Kesi's hair.

Spent hours making them bracelets (which they loved).

+ will ever love. Prefer mine with hooves.

Have hidden some prawns in the pocket of Christabel Cardew's hacking jacket. They'll be minging by the time she finds them. Everyone at riding school will think she has BO. Have hugged Sausage & Beans and fed them the asparagus Mum was saving for her farewell dinner tonight. It makes them fart – I hope Nelly suffers.

Kesi is taking me up to London to catch the train in an hour, so I've got to undo my suitcase and put my socks in and the other things I'm not allowed to take. Will write again when I'm on the train.

Dear Diary,

Am writing this in the ladies' at St Pancras Station. Have taken my tights off, flushed them down the pan and blocked the loo. Water is spilling over the bowl like Niagara Falls. Tried to mop it up with my beret but it's not v absorbent.

Kesi is waiting outside to hand me over to Miss Thomas, the teacher in charge of kids going to Blightleafe by train. Well, Miss Thomas will soon find out she's not the boss of me. Having a little boo now instead of when I have to say goodbye to Kesi in front of everyone. Don't want those little witches to see me cry.

Dear Diary,

I'm on the train sitting next to a girl called Hannah. She has cheeks like a hamster so that's what I'm calling her from now on – Hamster! She tried to suck up by offering me Haribo Starmix. When I said no, she said, 'Go on, it might make you sweeter.' The other girls laughed at me + her weak joke. Not talking to them now.

Just waved Kesi off. She said bye and told me to do my best but as she walked away, I leant out of train and yelled, 'I'll soon be back!' and

Hamster (Hannah) giggled like a ... squeaked, 'Ooh! Fancy saying *that*! ... long time you know.' Like I need ren... Can't stand her already.

Bit annoyed with Kesi too. She got all embarrassed just because I wouldn't shake hands with Miss Thomas – why should I? She's not the Queen. Kesi apologised for me in a v loud whisper and said it's because I'm an only child (good!) and very spoilt (not!) and that if she leaves me alone for a bit, I'll be all right. WRONG!

Miss M & D already. I know I'm mean to Mum sometimes and tease Dad but it's all done with love. Hope they weren't hurt when I said I wanted Kesi to take me to station and not them. I wanted them here so much. I was just angry. Can't believe they didn't get that + come to wave me off. No one understands me.

Mum made my favourite cake to put in my tuck box. Dad gave me a framed family photo and a little one of Ross. Kesi gave me a lucky charm to remind me of her. It's a hippo. Hope it works but no luck so far. Hamster (Hannah – you've got who she is now, right?) has started a sing-song. If she tries to make me join in, I'll jump off this train while it's still moving.

Dear Diary,

Sitting at the back of the coach on my own. Had to get away from Hamster. She's already bezzy mates with another new girl called Ellie Marsden. See if I care. Going to write rude words on the steamy window.

There's another kid sitting on her own in the next aisle called Joanna Townsend. She doesn't seem to have any friends, probably because she looks so boring + miserable. She keeps puffing on a puffer thing and sniffing, which isn't very attractive. Think she's got a cold. I didn't sit with her in case I caught germs or sadness or frizzy hair. Feel a bit sorry for her though; I didn't see anyone come to wave her off.

How come the older girls manage to look so cool in this hideous Whyteleafe uniform? Probably because theirs fit them. Wish I could hang out with them instead of the bunch of silly looking babies in Year 7. Seems like all the mums with kids in my year rang each other up and said, 'Just for a laugh, let's pretend our children have got arms as long as gibbons and 54-inch waists and make them wear new blazers + skirts two sizes too big.'

The coach has stopped. Are we here? Woah . . . is that Whyteleafe? Doesn't look like a school. Looks like Ye Olde Country Mansion with a massive lawn + tennis courts etc. It's even got a flagpole with a flag. Probably a haunted dump inside though. The goons are getting off now – better go. Laters.

Dear Diary,

I'm in the Whyteleafe cloakroom. Been told to wash my hands before lunch even though they're perfectly clean. Miss Thomas has asked a girl called Mei Ling to show the new girls round, i.e. me, Melinda Cartwright – who I shall call Carthorse from now on because she's huge and snorts a lot – and Ellie Marsden, who has a whiney voice and is irritating beyond belief. She's chatting away to the others like she's known them for ever but no one's talking to me. Bet they're saying stuff behind my back. This is why I didn't want to come. Knew I'd hate everybody.

Dear Diary,

Writing this under the staircase. Feel a bit bloated. Just to let you know the stew and dumplings were OK but the conversation was pants. Hamster was banging on about the puppy she got for Easter. She said her dad hid it in a huge Easter egg and when she opened it, there was a shih-tzu inside. I made good joke about it not being house-trained. No one laughed except Joanna Townsend but it might have been wheezing, because she suffers from asthma.

I know this because a chubby lad called Harry Dunn said, 'Uh-oh! Mousie (meaning Joanna) has got a bit of cheese stuck!'

Then he grabbed her under the arms and tried to perform the Heimlich manoeuvre to stop her choking and the Head Boy (William Murricane) said, 'Harry Dunn! Let go of Joanna ... *now!* She's not choking, she's asthmatic.'

Then she started crying, so Miss Thomas took her outside. Ellie Marsden groaned, 'Oh, look at

Mousie, turning on the waterworks.'

I glared at her because Mousie (Joanna) was upset but Ellie just pulled a face and said, '*What?*' like she'd done nothing wrong.

Then a twit with too much hair gel called Rowan started boasting about the bike he got for Easter to try to outdo Hamster (Hannah) but it's not even a good make. I didn't say anything, I couldn't care less what they all got but Mei Ling tried to make me join in by asking what I got for Easter, the nosy minx. So I lied and said I got a pot-bellied piglet that looks just like Miss Thomas. I didn't realise I said it so loudly but Miss Thomas heard. She didn't tell me off but a really bossy Irish girl called Shauna with boobs like melons poked me with her fork and said if I wasn't new, I'd be sat on for saying that. Not by her, I hope. Would bring my dumplings back up.

A man with a beard just found me under the staircase. He's either the music teacher or a gangster carrying a violin case. Thought he was going to tell me off but he just said, 'Damn! You've found my secret hiding place.' He shook my hand and said, 'Mr Lewis. Head of Music. Pleased to meet you.' Then he strode off, whiffing faintly of Imperial Leather soap, like Grandad used to.

Going to check into my new room now.

Dear Diary,

I'm in Room 6, sitting on my bed behind the blue curtain. This 'dorm' (as Stormin' Shauna calls it) is bit like a prison only with pretty duvet covers. Have just arranged my photos, hair straighteners, lucky hippo, catapult, musical torch, lip salve, scrunchy, bubble-gum stash and nodding dog on top of my bedside cabinet.

Shauna said we're only allowed to put six things on display, but stuff her. They're my things – I'll put them where I like. It's bad enough having to share sleeping quarters with five other girls who are even worse than Nelly. I've given them all marks out of ten (10 = girls I hate most):

- Hannah 'Hamster' James: 10
- Melinda 'Carthorse' Cartwright: 10
- Mei Ling (probably a spy): 10
- Ellie 'Smellie' Marden: 10
- Joanna 'Mousie' Townsend: 9
- Shauna 'Stormin'' O'Sullivan: 100

Gave Shauna 100 because she's room monitor and thinks she's the boss just because she's older than us, but she has no people skills. First thing she said to me wasn't, 'Hello, Elizabeth, I like your hair.' No. What she said was, 'Are you the eejit who was rude to Miss Thomas?' When I told her I'll be as rude as I like and she can't stop me, she attacked me with her electric toothbrush. Then she told me to put my tights back on. When I said no, she pushed me on to my bed and pulled my socks off. She has biceps like a man.

I almost slapped her but I thought better of it, maybe the poor thing is on medication + forgot to take it. So I just said, 'Who put you in charge – the secret police?'

She replied, 'No, I was voted in by the other kids. If you dis me, I'll report you and you'll be fined, so you will!'

Apparently they have meetings here. Shauna said that the Head Boy + Girl make the rules – not the teachers. If we break them, kids on the jury decide how to punish us. Hope they haven't built gallows in the playground or I'm gonna swing.

I'm not sticking to their stupid rules. I'm not even allowed to keep my own money, which goes against my human rights. We all have to put it in a pot and are given £10 a week – what can you buy with £10 these days? *Nothing* in the shops I go to.

If we need something 'important', e.g. a new

tennis racquet, we can ask for it, but we might not get it. Good! Don't want a racquet. I want a new phone. How am I supposed to live without a mobile?

Ha! Just remembered I don't have to. Hid my old one in my washbag, wrapped in a flannel. Have just texted Uncle Ru to come and get me. He is a childless bachelor. If I stay with him, he can tell his friends at golf club that I'm his love child + kill the rumour about him and his flatmate, Sebastian, and we can all go to the ballet.

Everyone has gone down to the playroom to put their cakes in the cupboard. We're all supposed to share what's in our tuck box at tea time. I told them they can whistle. They are NOT having any of my cake. Mum made it all for me.

Hamster was so shocked, I thought she was going to explode. I didn't think not sharing was such a biggy but Shauna screeched at me like flimmin' banshee: 'I'm fed-up of you already,

Lizzy! Keep your cake. If it's as foul as you it'll poison us anyway.'

She is so judgemental. And she called me Lizzy. I'm not having that. I said, '*Lizzy?* Don't you dare call me Lizzy. No one's ever been allowed to call me that, except my grandad!'

'I bet that isn't the only name he calls you,' she said. I could have flushed her stupid head down the toilet for that remark. Would have done if Mousie (Joanna) hadn't locked herself in the loo. Not sure what she's doing in there. The taps are full on so she's either washing her knickers or trying to cover up her sobbing. Hope it's the knickers thing. I'd be crying too if I were her.

Not sure what to do now – run away, or go down for tea with all those losers and eat cake? Think I will go and eat cake + run away after. Can't run on an empty stomach. Luckily I've got a packet of cheesy puffs on standby in case I have to make quick exit from the dining hall.

Dear Diary,

I'm in the common room, waiting to see Miss Belle + Miss Best. Why do we have two headmistresses anyway? They must have heard I was coming and feel safer in pairs. They want to talk to all the new kids to get to know us. Well, they won't get to know me. I'm not stopping by for long.

Melinda Carthorse has already gone galloping in, so I am stuck here with Ellie Marsden. She's flirting outrageously with a boy called Kenji Nakahara, i.e. pretending to fall off the sofa and flashing her pants on purpose. Kenji is more interested in the dead moth he found in his Pot Noodle but the other new boy – Rowan McDonald – seems to think Marsden is the bee's bits.

At tea time, Rowan told everyone his dad is a chemist, so quick as flash, I started singing: 'Old Macdonald had a pharm . . . acy – e-i-e-i-o!' Instead of farm. Which is funny, yes? Was going to share that joke with everyone but nobody would share their cake with me so I didn't bother.

It's all Shauna's fault. She banged on the dining table and told the whole world I didn't want to share my cake, even though I'd just changed my mind. I don't care if people think I'm bad but I am not *mean*. I'm a loving + generous person! Tried to prove this by asking if anyone wanted some of my double choc gateau but Hamster stuck her tongue out + Carthorse pulled a face like I'd put pepper in her nosebag.

Not feeling sad cos of that though. Kenji just put some music on – 'Clair de Lune'. Don't care if it's nerdy to like classical stuff, I love it. It's the tune Mum hummed to me when I was baby and couldn't sleep. I want to go HOME and sleep in my own bed with my own guinea pigs/horse, even if he does have muddy hooves.

Bummer. Melinda Carthorse is back. My turn to go and meet Miss Belle and Miss Best. I asked Carthorse what they are like and she did a horsey snort and said Miss Belle is blonde and slim and 'rarly, rarly beautiful' and Miss Best 'looks like

36

her father's game keeper in drag but is rarly kind, actually'.

I said, 'In that case, I'll call them Miss Beauty and Miss Beast,' and Carthorse thought it was so knickers-wettingly funny, she reared up and whinnied. I think she's related to the royals. She's got the same voice. She's probably a cross between an Arabian stallion and a mule.

Dear Diary,

Am at the back of the school field sitting on a swing that some random boy just pushed me off for kicking him in the goolies. Sorry, but what does he expect if he stands in front of a moving object and tries to boss me about? According to him, I was supposed to be in bed by 8 p.m. and oooh . . . it was 8.15 p.m. so he's reporting me at the next school meeting for disobeying him.

I told him I don't give a stuff because he isn't my dad so he can't tell me what to do, but he reckoned he can, cos, 'Everyone voted for him to be a monitor.'

So I said, 'Yeah, because you look like a lizard.' That was when he went to strangle me and I accidentally booted him in his boy bits. He went down like a sack of spuds but, after making big fuss, he stopped rolling about in the grass, yanked my hair and shook me off the swing. Completely unprovoked. I really hope he does report me anyway. I want Beauty (pink cashmere jumper, matching lipstick, kitten heels) and the Beast (horns, man trousers, nervous tic) to know I meant what I said to them earlier. Which was:

- I hate Whyteleafe
- I want to go home
- I'm going to be as bad + horrid as possible till they send me home
- They can punish me as much they like, e.g. thumbscrews/rack/triple maths – I don't care

But instead of going nuts like normal adults, they laughed, which I wasn't expecting. It wasn't a witchy laugh, more tinkly + hooty like a happy fairy and a friendly troll sharing a joke. I seriously thought they were going to wee themselves.

Miss Beast told me I can misbehave as much as I like, it doesn't bother her. And Miss Beauty nodded and smiled, which makes them either properly nice or somewhat mad, yes? They said no matter what I do, they'll never punish me because they like to leave that to the children. Are they weird or just lazy? I'm so confused.

Miss Beauty said that I look like 'such a lovely girl' and that she can't believe I'm half as bad as I made out and that one day, I'll make them both very proud. PROUD?

No one's ever been proud of me before. Loved me, yes. But proud? No. Made me feel bit weepy. Didn't let it show though. Tough as old boots, me. It's quite hard not to like Miss Beauty + Miss Beast and I think they kind of like me too ... STOP RIGHT THERE! Pull yourself together, Elizabeth. Get a strop on! Throw a tanty. You have to make these two lovely darlings hate you or they'll never kick you out.

Going back to the dorm to put frogspawn in Shauna's contact lens case for a bit of light relief.

Dear Diary,

Writing this under the duvet. Everyone else is asleep. Am so lonely. Had a fight with Shauna earlier. Wicked Irish banshee gave me a major telling-off for being an hour late, then humiliated me by saying I can't count just because I put more than six things out on my cabinet.

Well, I can count. I got an A* from my private maths tutor before he had a nervous breakdown. I need more than six things out! They are all essential to my happiness + well-being, so I refused to put any away.

That did it. Shauna snatched them, including my unlucky lucky potamus, threw them in a big trunk and locked it. Then she sat on it with her big spuddy backside. I tried to pull her off but she's built like a trucker and wouldn't shift. She said, 'I'm not going anywhere . . . You can have your stuff back in the morning if you say sorry, Lizzy.'

I said, '*Lizzy?* I've told you once. It's *Elizabeth* to you!'

She just said, 'Calm down. You'll burst a blood vessel,' which is the most annoying thing anyone can say when you're angry.

I am NOT saying sorry to Shauna ever, so I screamed at her, 'I'll make you *pay* for this!' By which time all the other inmates had woken up and started chipping in.

Hamster (Hannah) was squeaking at me to say sorry because if I didn't 'I was only hurting myself'. Plus similar
New Age claptrap.

Carthorse started whinnying + snorting in agreement with Hamster but was kind of on my side, making signs behind Shauna's back.

Ellie Marsden just giggled like a lunatic and danced up and down while squeezing her spots.

Joanna 'Mousie' Townsend zipped her head inside her rabbit pyjama case + started whimpering because she hates confrontation.

Mei Ling fired up her Ladyshave + buzzed her armpits like nothing was happening.

I'd just got Shauna in a headlock when my washbag started buzzing on the basin. *Yay! A text from Uncle Ru?* I let go of Shauna's head and backed off casually to try to grab it, but her enormous bat ears heard it.

I panicked and blamed the buzzing on Mei Ling's Ladyshave but she'd switched it off and was plucking her eyebrows by then. Shauna pounced, found my phone wrapped in the flannel and held it up like a split poo bag.

The following conversation went like this:

Shauna: Jeepers, Mary and Joseph! What's *this*, Elizabeth?

Me: An electric face cloth.

Carthorse: Electric face cloth . . . neeeheee hee, hee!

Shauna: Don't get clever with me, Allen.

Me: But you make it so easy. Give me my phone back.

Shauna: No! It's against rules to have mobiles at Whyteleafe.

Me: Don't care. Give it back, thief! My uncle Ru is a solicitor.

Shauna: I don't care if he's the Pope. Hannah, get her off me!

Hamster: Let go of Shauna's dressing-gown cord, Elizabeth. You're only hurting yourself.

Me: Stop your hippy nonsense. She started it!

Mousie: Please don't fight. Why can't we all
            be friends?
Mei Ling: Do deep-breathing, Joanna ... and
            in ... and out ...
Mousie: Feel dizzy. Help ... I've gone
            blind ...

Mousie went all wobbly + almost fainted. I rushed to save her and that was when Shauna took advantage of my good nature and locked my phone in the trunk with Ross + my family + everything I love.

She's reporting me at the meeting on Monday – good! Hopefully they will throw me out after breakfast which will give me plenty of time to escape to Uncle Ru's and hole up there with my animals till M & D stop babooning about and come home.

Escape Plan:

10.30:   Sneak into dorm, jemmy trunk open, get stuff back.

10.45:   Pack case. Change out of uniform. Find scissors and make mask out of beret.

11.00:   Borrow bike + hit the road to station.

11.30:   Buy train ticket + sandwich + comic. Catch train to London.

13.30:   Call Uncle Ru + bribe him to pick me up from station.

14.00:   Rescue Sausage + Beans from Nelly hell.

14.30:   Fetch Ross, ride him to Uncle Ru's + park him in garden.

15:00:   Afternoon tea with Uncle Ru + Sebastian.

17:00:   Matinee with Uncle Ru to see Sebastian in *Swan Lake*.

18:00:   Feed + groom + cuddle animals.

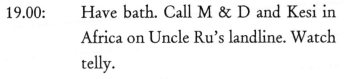

19.00:	Have bath. Call M & D and Kesi in Africa on Uncle Ru's landline. Watch telly.
22.00:	Go to bed.

That's the plan. But what if it wasn't Uncle Ru who texted me? What if it was just an ad for cheap cinema tickets? Or what if it *was* Uncle Ru texting to say he doesn't want me to come live with him because he needs his space/I'm such bad person?

I'll never know now. My phone will be dead by morning.

Miss you, Ross, and your horsey kisses.

Miss you, Sausage, and the little *wheep-wheep* noise you make when you greet me.

Miss you, Beans, with your baked-bean fur + Elvis quiff + way you smell of hay.

Miss you, Kesi, because you're like my second mum.

Miss you, Mum, because even though you're

annoying, you're lovely + clever + beautiful + wouldn't swop you for the world.

Miss you, my brilliant, hilarious, badly dressed daddy.

Do any of you miss me?

SUNDAY

Dear Diary,

No lessons today. Went for walk by myself as no one is speaking to me. Mousie (Joanna) tried but she has such soft little voice, it was hard to tell what she was going on about. So I just said, 'Eh?' and she said, 'N-nothing.' Like she was a bit scared. Not sure what her problem is. She's not a happy bunny. It's bugging me, seeing her like that. If she were a real mouse and a cat was after her, I'd rescue her and keep her safe in my pocket.

But she isn't a mouse and right now, I've got problems of my own.

Didn't put frogspawn in Shauna's contact lens case after all. It seemed mean to the developing tadpoles so I put it back in the pond. I got my revenge though. Found Shauna's bra and ran it up the flagpole. It looks like a giant lace windsock. She hasn't noticed yet. But she will.

Had a wander round the school garden. There's a big veg patch + loads of flower beds. I love growing stuff. I'll often help Grandma at her allotment. When I get angry, digging calms me down, so G'ma gave me my own patch. Last year, I dug up all the weeds + grew lettuces, radishes, runner beans + pumpkins the size of my head. I even grew sweet peas and made a wigwam out of canes for them to climb up. Grandad used to grow them, so I thought, why not?

Met a boy in the school garden. His name is John Terry but everyone calls him JT for short. Think he's the head gardener cos he was making a really good wigwam for the sweet pea seedlings he's grown in the greenhouse. He didn't say much, just smiled then kept planting. Didn't mind him not talking. I just liked watching him work. Don't know why. He seems older than he looks – sort of gentle + wise.

Not that I fancy him! I just think he might make a good friend who isn't a girl. Not that I need friends, of course. But if I did.

I asked him if he'd soaked his sweet pea seeds

to help them germinate and he said, 'Aye . . . Keen gardener, are you? I could do with an assistant. Maybe put your name down at the next meeting?'

'No point,' I said. 'I'm not staying. I hate Whyteleafe.'

He looked surprised but said, 'Ah well. Please yourself, Elizabeth.' I never told him my name so I asked how he knows who I am. 'Everyone knows,' he said. 'You're the naughtiest girl in the school – or are you?'

'You'd better believe it!' I said. Then I kicked his bucket over to prove it. I LOVE being the naughtiest girl in school. I earned that reputation in just one day – genius! I was all ready for JT to ram the bucket over my head and put a worm down my hoody. But he didn't. He did something worse.

He said, 'I get it. You're homesick. It's OK.'

Don't know why it upset me so much but it did. So I yelled at him. Really yelled. 'You don't know me!' Then I told him where to stick his sweet peas. That showed him.

Dear Diary,

Midnight. Wide awake. While I was with JT, Shauna threaded all my pants on a hockey stick and hung them out of the dorm window in the rain. So now everyone's seen my underwear and I haven't got any dry ones for tomoz. Everyone thinks Shauna is soooo clever for getting her own back on me. Well ha-dee ha. I don't care. They can gang up on me as much as they like, I shan't behave.

Wish I hadn't shouted at JT though. He probably hates me now. Not that I fancy him. Even though he has got eyes like a husky + strong hands + a cute accent. Don't fancy him though. Not one bit.

He's feeble. That's what he is. He's FEEBLE for not chasing me with his watering can + pouring it over my head. That's what I'd do if someone kicked my bucket over.

Got my first lesson tomorrow. Dreading it. Am in Miss Ranger's class. Overheard Carthorse saying that Miss Ranger is a prize mare – and she should know. What if she makes me sit next to JT?

M☹NDAY

Dear Diary,

So far, so bad. I'm on the naughty step outside Miss Ranger's classroom. She threw me out. All I did was ping my rubber at Hamster's head + flick a few pellets around. Oh, and I hummed a bit and swung on my chair. What did she expect? It's her silly fault for letting me sit at the back of class.

Had been good all morning, i.e. got sums + spellings right, because I'm not thick. The trouble was, Miss Ranger wrote 'Excellent' on all my work and I thought, *PANTS! How can I be naughtiest girl in school if I get good marks?*

So I started messing about. Miss Ranger ignored me for ages, so I had to up my game. Made a blowpipe out of a biro + fired some ink pellets, one of which landed on her desk.

'WHO DID THAT?' bellowed Miss Ranger.

Mei Ling was busy filing her nails so she didn't see me do it.

Ellie Marsden grassed me up straightaway, but to my great happiness, she got told off for telling tales.

Rowan poked me in the back with a set square + told me to fess up or we'd all get in trouble.

Mousie was having kittens + pleading with me to own up with her big watery eyes.

I was going to say it was me all along. I just wanted to see how the other kids reacted. Know your enemies, Elizabeth. That's what Kesi always says.

I put my hand up and said, 'It was me, Miss!' and Miss Ranger said that if I was that bored, I could sit outside until I was *less* bored because I was 'spoiling it for the rest of the class'.

Excuse me but it's not *me* who's spoiling it, it's her! Since when was making us do maths a treat? The other kids must lead sad lives if algebra = highlight of their day.

I was actually making the school day more fun for them. Carthorse was snickering away like anything when my rubber pinged off Hamster's skull.

And I saw Harry Dunn pull his biro apart to copy my blowpipe design. Even JT smiled. His desk is in front of mine by the window. He has a nice smile if you like that sort of thing. Which I don't.

Between you + me, lessons are much more fun here than at home. I only had my tutors to annoy before. Now I've got a whole class full of kids and Miss Ranger to rub up the wrong way!

Bit bored now, sitting out here all on my own. My tights are rubbing. I had put socks on first thing this morning. Shauna didn't notice but Hamster spotted them at breakfast and shouted across the hall so everyone could hear.

'How sweet! Elizabeth Allen is wearing socks like she's in the infants. Shauna, ask Miss Best and Miss Belle to let her keep them on because she's such a big baby.' Everyone started laughing

+ pointing until Rebekah Shah (Head Girl) reminded them I'm new and it's their job to make me feel welcome. Told her I don't need her sticking up for me and ran off.

Yes, OK, I have put my tights on now. But not because of what Hamster said. I put them on because it's a bit chilly in a kilt. Especially when wearing pants left out in the rain. Trust me. Mr Lewis just bumbled by and asked why I'm not in class. When I told him, he said, 'Hmm. I'm guessing you're a creative type, in which case you won't want to miss the next lesson. It's art.'

Art is one of my favourite subjects. Before my private art tutor went on permanent sick leave, she said I should go abroad to study. She said the more miles between us, the more I'd grow as an artist and suggested a five-year painting course in Outer Mongolia.

Don't want to miss art lesson. Going back into class to paint a masterpiece.

Dear Diary,

Here's why I don't like Monday:

I said sorry to Miss Ranger but she said it was too late for me to do any painting and made me do more maths.

Shauna still won't let me have my stuff back because I won't say sorry but I need my hair straighteners to dry my pants as the radiator is off.

Asked Ellie v politely if I could borrow her hairdryer to dry my pants and she said no, put fingers down her throat and pretended to gag. So I borrowed it while she was at choir practice.

I only used it on the highest setting for about an hour but then it went *BANG* + smoke came out + it broke. Not my fault if Ellie brings dangerous electrical equipment into school, is it?

Could have had an electric shock and got Uncle Ru to sue her but I know she'll blame me + bring it up at the stupid meeting and they'll make me buy her a new hairdryer.

Then I will have to pretend I've got no money and they'll all pity me for being poor even though I've got £25 stashed inside my *Book of Reptiles and Amphibians* plus vouchers for a double meat feast pizza + fries + Fanta.

Dear Diary,

There is no justice in this world. Not at Whyteleafe anyhow. Just got back from my first meeting. I knew it would be a disaster letting kids be the judge. They're far more evil than teachers, I swear.

We went over all the rules again – hand over all cash + no going down to the village on your own + do as the monitors tell you + do not commit murder, yada-yada-yada. Nearly fell asleep it was so boring. Rebekah Shah (Head Girl) is quite cool and Will Murricane (Head Boy) has good hair + bit of stubble going on but *don't* get me started on the jury.

There are twelve of them, all completely insane and in need of lobotomies. Don't know who most of them are and don't care, but Shauna is on the jury and the boy I kicked in the goolies, so I knew I was in big trubs the minute the meeting started.

I brought my purse along as I thought I'd go and redeem my pizza voucher in the village at break, but they probably haven't got Pizza Hut in Frampshire. It'll be all niminy-piminy tea shops + fusty boutiques selling old-lady-stylee thermal vests + long johns.

When it came to collecting our money, I quickly sat on my purse. Then a monitor called Thomas wandered up and down asking everyone to flash their cash, but when he shook the money box at me I blanked him. He looked at me strangely but didn't say anything so thought I'd got away with it. But when he'd finished doing his rounds, I saw him whispering to the Head Boy.

Next thing, William Murricane banged on the table with his hammer like he was whacking a gigantic nail in. When everyone stopped nattering he said, 'Elizabeth Allen didn't put any money in the box.'

Mousie was trembling from the hammer blows, puffing on her inhaler and gasping, 'Elizabeth. Please, please don't get into trouble. I hate it when everyone shouts.'

So I didn't shout. Just called out, 'Yes, Willy. I have got money but I'm keeping it.'

Everyone went 'Whoa!' and 'Willy?' Then of all the cheek, Willy Murricane told me to stand up when he's talking to me, like he's GOD. Gone right off him. He's full of wind, is William Murricane. So from now on, he is Windy Hurricane.

I just sat there with my arms crossed but then Hamster – who was sitting behind me – jabbed me in the bum and I leapt up in shock, which is when she grabbed my purse and started waving it in the air and gibbering like she'd got free tickets to La La Land.

Windy Hurricane asked why I want to keep the money to myself and when I said, 'Duh! To buy stuff,' he made a long speech because he *really* loves the sound of his own voice.

'At Whyteleafe School – blah la blah – we don't like to think that some of us have lots of money when others have hardly any (*sob, weep, violin music*) so we all get the same and if you want anything extra you can have it if the meeting agrees.'

Hamster actually clapped, which annoyed me hugely. Even though I totally got what Windy was wittering on about, it isn't going to work for me. I explained this v clearly to him. I said, 'Listen up, Windy. I'm not putting my money in the box because . . .'

- I'm not staying in this dump long enough to get a good return on my investment

- £10 a week is diddly-squat
- I need my money for the train fare home when finally expelled

For some reason this caused a massive buzz. Mr Johns (in charge of the boys) almost had a coronary, Miss Beauty distracted herself by adjusting her bra strap and Miss Beast's eye went into twitch-mode.

The Head Boy + Girl had a good old mutter, then Windy Hurricane got his hammer out again and went *CRASH* on the table so hard I thought the legs were going to fall off. When everyone shut up, he started going on and on about me like he's my mum.

'We think Elizabeth is wrong and silly.' (I tell you what's silly, Windy – the way you tuck your school jumper into your trousers.)

'Her parents are paying a lot of money (they can afford it) to keep her in this fine school.' (It's not fine and I never asked to come here.)

'Even if she does leave early (don't ever doubt it) her term fee still has to be paid.' (So? Peanuts compared to going to Africa.)

'Also, we think she is very feeble not to try to see if she likes Whyteleafe.' (No, you're feeble for staying here so long – it stinks.)

I didn't say that stuff in brackets. I just thought it. What I actually said was, 'If I'm not expelled, I'll run away.' I meant every word.

BUT . . . Diary, they took my own money off me! Windy told Hamster to bring my purse to the front and she gave me a smug look, skipped up to the desk and emptied every penny into the box.

As if that wasn't bad enough, some muppet called Maurice stood up and said he doesn't think I should be given any pocket money at all this week because of my behaviour. Then all the jury put their hands up and voted against me, the miserable baa lambs.

Rebekah Shah (Head Girl, willowy, good with eyeliner) saw I was upset and tried to be the

nice guy. She said she knows I am finding things tough and if I have a good report next week, all will be forgiven and I'll get my £10, but I was in *such* a rage, I felt like snatching Windy's hammer and smashing my way out.

Stormin' Shauna made a BIG show of dishing out money to everyone except me and said, 'You're a fool, so you are, Elizabeth. Stop making things so hard for yourself, why don't you?'

I'm not making things hard for myself – *she* is! I knew the minute Windy Hurricane asked if anyone had any other complaints she'd tell him about me running her bra up the flagpole etc. I'd put money on it if they hadn't taken it off me. Only she *didn't* mention it. Nor did the monitor boy who I kicked. Which is v odd. Maybe it's because they're embarrassed – Shauna cos her bra cups are bigger than my rucksack and monitor boy because he got googlied by an eleven-year-old girl.

But what if the reason they didn't report me

is because I'm new + deserve a chance. Is that their little game – to be nice so I *like* them? I'm not falling for that old trick or I'll never get expelled. I'll be stuck here for years . . . waaaaghhh!

Tuesday

Dear Diary,

Everyone has gone off without me. Melinda Carthorse and Ellie Marsden are playing tennis. Hamster and Rowan have gone down to village to 'buy sweets', or so they say. Mei Ling is practising kung fu in the woods and Shauna has gone to the dentist, hopefully to get her mouth sewn up.

Don't know where Mousie is. Wonder if Joanna minds being called Mousie? It can be a bad or a good thing, can't it? Like super-cute and dinky, or plain and timid. Maybe it depends who says it. I loved it when Grandad called me Lizzy. Not Shauna though. She hasn't earned the right.

Anyway, I think I've upset Mousie or Joanna or whatever she wants to be called. She asked if I'd go to the village with her and I said, 'What's the point, I've got no money.' So I don't think she had anyone to go with. Feel bad about that, but if everyone's being mean to me – why should I be any different?

Bored, bored, bored, bored, bored. Could go to garden to see John Terry and apologise for telling him where to stick his sweet peas, maybe? Na. Not doing that. Will make me look weak and pitiful.

Dear Diary,

Glad everyone left me alone now cos I just had a BRILLIANT piano lesson with Mr Lewis. I was wandering about by the music room when I heard him playing a piece which sounded like a storm at sea with thunder + waves crashing. I could almost SMELL the seaweed. He caught me listening and asked if I can play the piano. 'Yes, I'm quite good at tinkling the ivories, sir,' I said.

I'd have got my Grade 4 if my private music tutor hadn't hurt her fingers. Nothing to do with me, I swear. She did it to herself on purpose. I was fiddling with the metronome when suddenly she went nuts + slammed the piano lid down on her own fingers. She never came back after that. Shame, as I wanted to learn the violin.

Anyway, it seems I'm down for music lessons with Mr Lewis. He said he'll teach me the sea piece but when I told him I'm leaving Whyteleafe, he said it's a waste of time teaching it to me and went to cross me off his list. This upset me no end, so I said, 'Can't I have just a few lessons till I go, sir? Please! I'm a very quick learner.'

Bless him, he said he had twenty minutes to spare and gave me a music sheet with a tricky piece by Handel. 'I can handle Handel, sir,'

I said, because I learnt that one for Grade 4.

After I played it, Mr Lewis shouted, 'Bravo!' got v excited and told me I have a real talent and that it's a shame I want to leave because I'd be one of his best pupils.

I said, 'I was going to run away today, but they took my money off me so I can't pay for the train ticket. Could you lend me twenty quid for the fare, sir? My dad will pay it back when he's finished studying baboons. He's loaded.'

For some reason Mr Lewis thought that was hilarious and started spluttering into his hanky and saying, 'Oh, you are such an *enfant terrible* . . . yet you play like an angel! Off you go . . . off! Off!'

BUT he did say I can have another lesson on Friday – if I haven't been expelled. So I might hang around till then. See how it goes.

I like Mr Lewis even though he has got scrambled egg in his beard.

Wednesday

Dear Diary,

Just back from a riding lesson. I don't need lessons as I've been riding for donkey's years so I was allowed to gallop once we got off the bridle track. I was on a pony called Smokey. Don't know why he's called Smokey. He isn't grey + doesn't smoke as far as I know. Ellie thinks she's a good rider but she's rubbish – she couldn't ride a bus.

The riding instructor gave her an old plodder called Dickens and every time it walked, it farted.

PARP!

I kept pretending it was her: 'Phoarr! Excuse you, Smellie Marsden!'

And she kept saying, 'Shut up! It's not me, it's Dickens!' but no one believed her and now everyone's calling her Smellie Marsden, which serves her right for being born.

It was nice riding in the countryside. But it made me miss Ross even more. Do hope he's thrown Christabel Cardew in the water trough. Wonder if she's found the minging prawns I hid in her pocket yet?

Mr Lewis is holding a music concert tonight for anyone who's interested. Might pop my head in, got nothing else to do.

Dear Diary,

Went to Mr Lewis's concert. No one from my class was there (good!), apart from Harry Dunn. He was only there because it was raining and he wanted to get out of rugby practice. Said he'd sprained his ankle but I saw him running down the corridor like a chubby cheetah earlier with Smellie Marsden charging after him yelling, 'Kiss me! Slow down! Why won't you kiss me?' Felt sorry for him. She terrorises the boys.

She's got a photo of her favourite boy band by her bed and slobbers all over it, spreading germs.

The concert was great. Mr Lewis played the violin like Yehudi.

Note to self: *Ask school jury for money to buy Stradivarius violin so Mr Lewis can teach me how to play it.*

I said that to him as a joke after the concert and he said I can always borrow a violin + he'll be happy to teach me. HAPPY? No one's ever been *happy* to teach me before! Maybe it's because Mr Lewis is a better teacher than the others. He even wrote down the name of the sea music I love ('Opus 55') and said I can get a great recording of it at the mini WHSmith in the village. I can listen to it whenever and it will help me practise.

When I reminded him I have no money, he said if I'm good, even if the jury refuse to cough up thousands of pounds for a Stradivarius, they might give me money to buy the DVD instead.

'Don't say it's just for you, say it's for everyone to enjoy,' he suggested. Then he tapped his nose and something shot out of his nostril. I didn't laugh though because stuff like that happens when you're old and I didn't want to embarrass him. He so reminds me of Grandad, my oldest, best and only real friend. My soulmate.

Wish he was still around. He'd never have let them send me to this hell hole. Still cry for him. This Saturday, it will be three whole years since he died. How come it still hurts like yesterday?

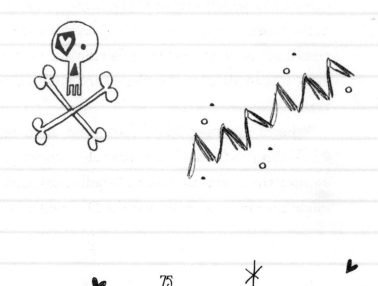

THURSDAY

Dear Diary,

I've got a new nickname. Don't know whether to be angry/pleased. Miss Ranger was taking us for history and when she asked Rowan McDonald if he could tell her anything about Elizabeth the First he said, 'No, miss, but I can tell you about Elizabeth the Worst.' And pointed at me with his ruler. Everyone thought that was just brilliant. Smellie Marsden nearly fell off her chair cackling and Carthorse was wheezing like she'd just won the Grand National. Even Kenji who's a terrible swot put his head in his desk so Miss Ranger couldn't see he was laughing.

Miss Ranger got all sarcastic and shouted, 'Well, I'm glad you find Elizabeth's bad behaviour so amusing. You won't be laughing when you fail your exams + can't get jobs + end up living

76

underneath the arches because Elizabeth Allen kept interrupting lessons and stopped you from—'

'I *didn't* interrupt, miss!' I was just sitting quietly writing to M & D and Kesi.

'There you go again,' she said. 'Interrupting! Much as I disapprove of name-calling, I can see why Rowan said that clever play on words. You really are the worst child I've ever taught, Elizabeth.'

'Why hasn't the bell gone, miss?' said Harry Dunn. 'Only it's lunch time according to your clock.'

'Maybe Elizabeth the Worst broke the bell,' squeaked Hamster.

I didn't touch the bell, fools! I moved the clock hand forward. Oldest trick in the book and they all fell for it.

Miss Ranger only realised what had happened when the whole class arrived in the dining hall half an hour before the dinner ladies were expecting us and sent us back.

Everyone guessed I'd done it. I didn't deny it as they were all so pleased to escape from history lesson. Backfired though. Miss Ranger made everyone go to lunch late to make up for lost time so they missed out on break. Now they really do think I'm Elizabeth the Worst, the snivelling hypocrites.

FRIDAY

Dear Diary,

Can't believe I've been at Frighteleafe for a whole week. Just in bed in my PJs eating gummy bears that I found loose under Carthorse's bed. Bit hairy but I ran them under the tap and they're fine. I left the school dance early cos Smellie Marsden was annoying me. She kept swishing her hair like she's Britain's Next Top Model and pretending to be squiffy on wine gums.

Then she started strutting her funky stuff at JT and she was getting right in his face so I stood between them and threw some crazy shapes right in *her* face to see how much she liked it. Which was not a lot, because I accidentally whacked her Coke out of her hand with one of my groovier moves, and she was wearing a white top.

She had complete hissy fit. Don't know why. I did her a favour – it's a hideous top and Coke washes out if you use Biotex. And anyway, who wears a boob tube these days, apart from my mum?

John left after that. Probably because the music was rubbish.

SATURDAY

Dear Diary,

I woke up late. Carthorse kept me awake farting. Been thinking about Grandad and feeling sad. He had a piano in his bungalow. I used to sit next to him on the piano stool when I was little and he taught me to play 'Chopsticks' + 'Trot, Trot, Trot' + 'Frere Jacques' etc.

Going to ask Shauna if I can go to the village and see if they've got the sea music Mr Lewis told me about. Can't buy it yet as still got no money but I could ask the shopkeeper to save it for me.

Wonder if Mousie will come with me? I'll ask. Only I'm not sure where she's gone. To see if the postman's been maybe. Mei Ling said Mousie never gets letters. Methinks she might be an orphan. I got a letter from G'ma yesterday. Maybe I'll get one from M & D/Kesi today. Will go down and see.

Dear Diary,

Sitting on a log on my way to the village. Shauna said I could go as long as I went with someone but nobody would come.

Mei Ling said she 'had to be somewhere' but wouldn't say where. (Told you she was a spy.)

Carthorse said she's going swimming with Hamster.

Smellie Marsden said she wouldn't go anywhere with me if I was last person on earth because I scared JT off at the dance.

Mousie said she's too scared to go with me in

case I get us banned from the village then burst into tears as she hasn't got a single letter and I've got two – one from M & D and one from Kesi – which I'm saving to read at bedtime.

So I'm going to the village on my own.

Dear Diary,

Sitting outside Ye Olde Tea Shop. Rebekah Shah came out of WHSmith just as I was going in. Thought I was in BIG trubs because I was on my own which isn't allowed till I'm in Year 10.

She was really nice though. When I told her no one would come with me she said she can't believe *nobody* likes me and asked if I'm really that bad? I said I *have* to be a total nightmare or Miss Beauty and Miss Beast won't send me home and she said, 'But if you're nice to people, they'll be nice back and you'll make friends and won't be so unhappy. It's really good at Whyteleafe. Honest.'

She bought me hot chocolate and a bun with

her own money. Gave her the silent treatment even so. I don't need her charity or her pity. Nice bun though. Lots of currants.

She kept yacking and said, 'It's not just you you'll make unhappy. Your M & D will be really upset + embarrassed if you get expelled. You don't really want to hurt them, do you?'

I wasn't having her think that so said, 'No, course I don't! It's not about them, it's about me. I don't mind ME hurting but I'd never hurt *them*. I can't bear it when *anyone's* sad. It really cuts me up.'

'I believe you,' she said. 'You're lovely really, I can tell. I know you're just putting on a front.' Nearly started blubbing then. Styled it out by pretending I'd choked on my bun. Not sure she fell for it though. Said she'd give me some space while she went to the chemist to get girly stuff.

When she came back, she said something I didn't expect. 'If you mean what you said about it cutting you up when other people are sad, would you do me a favour, Elizabeth. Will you make friends with Joanna Townsend? She's v unhappy. More than you'd ever know.'

I said, 'What, you mean Mousie?'

'Yeah, but if I tell you why, promise you'll keep it to yourself? I'm the only one who knows because we live on the same street and my mum told me.'

I promised.

Don't tell a soul, Diary but Mousie is glum because she thinks her mum and dad don't love her. They never write or visit and she's scared to make friends in case they ask her to stay for a sleepover and her mum doesn't return the favour – in which case she'd die of shame.

I'm not having that! Poor, poor Mousie. No wonder she's quiet like she is. I've vowed to Rebekah that I'll be Mousie's friend + protector. If anyone upsets her, they will have ME to answer to.

Dear Diary,

Am in the common room listening to music. Just had lunch. Pasta and treacle sponge. Got custard down my tie. Stormin' Shauna collared me and asked if I went to village on my own. Said YES. Didn't tell her I was with Rebekah – none of her business. She's reporting me at next meeting but I don't care.

Tried to sit next to Mousie at lunch but Carthorse's big backside was in the way so I couldn't. Noticed Mousie didn't eat anything. Not a good sign. She's just walked into the common room. Think I'll ask her to come to Mr Lewis's concert with me tonight. He holds them every Wed + Sat so at least I've got something fun to do.

Dear Diary,

Still in the common room. Just asked Mousie to come to the concert and the cheeky minx blew me out! Said she's got a letter to write. She's always writing letters. Will try to persuade her later. Just going to tell Mr Lewis I'm coming to his concert, maybe with Mousie, maybe not.

Dear Diary,

Don't know what to do! Asked Mousie to the concert again and she was all on her own, sobbing into her writing set. It broke my heart seeing her like that. Asked her what was up but she accused me of spying on her. Then she said, 'I suppose you'll tell everyone I've been crying now.'

I said, 'I'd never do that. Please believe me, Mousie – can I call you Mousie? I'm not half as horrible as I make out. I'm a bit bad maybe, but it's for a reason. It's not personal except with Shauna and she started it. Let's be friends.

Go on. What do you say?'

And she said, 'I don't care what you call me. Go awaaaaay!'

I am NOT giving up on her though.

Dear Diary,

Back in the dorm. The concert was good but I couldn't enjoy it as kept thinking about Mousie. Was going to try and talk to her but she went to bed early. Lots of wet tissues on her cabinet. More than six. Surprised Shauna didn't give her a mouthful. Going to read my letters from M & D and K, and then sleep. Night-night.

SUNDAY

Dear Diary,

Been up half the night with Mousie. Heard her crying so crept into her cubicle, sat on her bed and asked her what was wrong – was she homesick? I begged her to tell me and promised not to laugh or tell anyone else. I just wanted to help.

She told me to go away again but I said no because she was still sobbing so she clearly needs someone, and it might as well be me, because I haven't got anyone either.

Told her I know how she feels. I'm unhappy too because of not going to Africa + missing M & D, K, Ross, Saus and Beans but she started ranting, 'You don't know how lucky you are! You got a letter from your M & D, didn't you? I didn't. I never do! I bet yours had loads of kisses on the bottom, didn't it? Because they

88

really love you. Mine don't and I don't even know why. I don't know *whhhhhy*!'

So I hugged her and she cried and cried till she got it all out. Apparently it's her birthday soon and she's worried she won't get a present, cake or even a card. The others tease her about it. It got so bad she sent a letter to herself once, but one of the boys found out and she never lived it down. I asked her which boy and told her I'd throttle him with my bare hands, but she wouldn't say.

'I'm so jealous of you, Elizabeth!' she sobbed. 'You're as bad as anything but your M & D and Queasy *still* love you. I try to be good. I send loving letters + get good grades + never ask for anything or make a fuss but you are loved and I'm not. It's so unfair!'

I started sobbing too because I felt so guilty for being a spoilt brat. I told her I'd share everything with her and that she's sweet + kind and I can't understand why her parents are so mean.

'It's *them*, not you, Mousie,' I said. 'Maybe

they're having marriage problems. Has your mum got a fit milkman?'

But that upset her even more and she said, 'Oh noo! You think they're getting a divorce?'

I said probably not, but stuff happens. And even if they do split up, it isn't the end of world. She's got me now. I'll be there for her. Friends for ever.

'You're going though, aren't you?' she said.

'Not yet matey.' I squeezed her hand and she squeezed mine back, and said I'm not Eliz the Worst really. Mousie said she knows that now and thanked me for being a friend.

Thank you too, Mousie. Big time.

Dear Diary,

Mousie wants to see photos of my folks + animals but they're still locked in Shauna's Naughty Trunk. Much as I don't want to, I will have to apologise to her (agggghhh!) for putting more than six things out, or I will never get my stuff back.

Massive deal as I never back down. Am putting my bad reputation on the line here, for Mousie.

Dear Diary,

Got my stuff back. Weirdly, Shauna didn't gloat. She was quite ☺ when I asked and said, 'Sure you can, Elizabeth. Sorry always makes it right – unless you set fire to the sports pavilion in which case . . . not!'

So she does have a sense of humour. Didn't give me back my phone but hey, that was never gonna happen. Mousie helped me choose six things to leave out in order of importance:

1. Family photo
2. Photo of Ross
3. Lucky hippo
4. Musical torch
5. Lip salve
6. Bubblegum

Was going to substitute catapult for lip salve but Mousie said it looked a bit cluttered so I bunged it in a drawer. Showed her my pics of M & D, K and Ross. She wanted to know all about them and asked me to read my letter to her. Here are the highlights:

- They miss me terribly (tick)
- They hope I have made nice friends (tick)
- It's very hot in Africa (duh)
- Baboon mating behaviour varies greatly depending on the social structure of the group (ooh-err!)
- Dad's got diarrhoea (ugh!)
- They love me loads (tick)

Then I read her Kesi's letter which was mostly about her baby grandson. She still loves me best though. Natch. Kesi's letter highlights:

- Bubba Tundi is the apple of her eye (pah!)
- He's got such a cute little face + bum +

nose (aww!)

- He's got his grandma Kesi's good looks + intelligence (?!)
- He's a good boy, not like some children (pah!)
- I will always be her best baby girl (woo-hoo!)
- My father is full of diarrhoea (no change there then!)

MONDAY

Dear Diary,

Here's what Elizabeth the Worst did today:

1. Got sent out of class by M'selle Dupont for singing rude song, even though I sang it in perfect French.

2. Helped Harry Dunn button his blazer up right over his head in history so he looked like he'd been guillotined by Marie Antoinette.
3. Used Hamster's beret as a fishing net when we went pond-dipping in biology.
4. Got told off by Miss Beast for tying my tie in a trendy way, even though her flies were undone.
5. Got told off by Miss Beauty for not tucking my blouse in, even though she had a bit of lipstick on her teeth.

Here's what Elizabeth the Best did:

1. Helped Mr Lewis up when he fell backwards over his briefcase.
2. Rescued a caterpillar from Harry Dunn's salad at lunch and released it back into the wild.

3. Told Mousie v quietly that her skirt was tucked into her pants after PE.

4. Handed Carthorse some bog roll in the girls' toilet because she'd run out.

5. Stuck up for Mousie when Smellie Marsden teased her about not getting a letter again. Told her Mousie has four letters and a cheque *actually*, you stupid ignoramus. So I lied. Don't care. Made Mousie feel good and wiped the silly grin off Smellie's face.

Tuesday

Dear Diary,

Had a dream about JT last night. Told Mousie and she said that means I like him and should say sorry for kicking his bucket over. I said I might do as I quite like him, but only like a brother. She asked me if I miss not having any brothers and sisters and I said not as much as I miss having a grandad. She asked me why I loved him so much. So I made a list:

1. He sang me marching songs when I walked on my stilts.
2. He let me rub magic hair-restorer on his bald head which I made from rose petals + earwigs + rainwater.
3. He bought me pic 'n' mix + plasticine + colouring books + plastic animals for my toy farm.
4. He sat on end of my bed + read me stories when I had chickenpox.
5. He pushed my doll's pram for me when I was tired.
6. He taught me how to tie my shoelaces.

A thousand things really. Never mind. Love you, Grandad.

Wednesday

Dear Diary,

Went swimming today. My team won the relay – woo-hoo! Never been in a real race before unless you count that time when I was four and forced Kesi to play horses in the garden.

Got told off after by the lifeguard for running round the pool and doing a victory dance. Why do grown-ups always tell us off for running? They're the fun police.

Bit of a drama when Harry Dunn dive-bombed into the shallow end by mistake. He didn't hurt himself as he has a very thick head but his trunks came off. Smellie Marsden rescued them and put them on a polystyrene float so it looked like it was wearing pants but when she let go, it bobbed off to the deep end, and the lifeguard had to get his hook and fish them out. I almost drowned laughing. Carthorse peed herself. She denied it but the water level definitely rose and it was a lot warmer where she was standing.

Held Mousie's towel up for her when we got dressed in the communal changing room because she's shy. She needs a bra but doesn't want to ask her mum and can hardly ask the jury at the next meeting. Can you imagine the tittering? Might ask Rebekah in private if she can let Mousie have bra money from school funds.

Carthorse has no shame + prances around in the nuddy like no one's looking. She doesn't care who sees because her parents are naturists. Mine are naturalists. Only difference (apart from two letters) is that Carthorse's M & D look ridiculous without clothes on and mine look ridiculous with clothes on. Which is worse? Do the maths.

Parents + clothes or − clothes = equally embarrassing.

Carthorse is a good swimmer though. Thighs like trees. Hands like hams. She's 'a strapping

lass' as G'ma would say and 'a jolly good sport'.
Can't remember why I didn't use to like her now.

THURSDAY

Dear Diary,

Just re-read last few entries. Sounds a bit too
much like I'm enjoying myself. I am NOT! Well,
maybe a bit, but I still want to go home, so I will
have to start messing about more + annoying
everyone, except Mousie, of course.

Mousie doesn't want me to leave but I think if
I can get her confidence up a bit, she'll be OK.
Got a few weeks till half-term, but I have to be
gone by then. Might have to lasso Carthorse and
persuade her to be Mousie's new BF when I get
expelled. I'm sure they'll trot along v happily.
Hmm. Hope they don't in a way as makes me
feel bit jealous. Dunno. Will sort it somehow . . .

Won't be able to leave happy if I know Mousie is sad and alone. Maybe I'll ask Mum if we can adopt her and she can be my step-mouse.

FRIDAY

Dear Diary,

Did good job of winding Miss Ranger up today. Should be back on track for getting chucked out. She had to punish me five times, see below.

Ranger Punishments:

1. Made me stay behind and wipe off the hilarious portrait I drew of her on the whiteboard even though it showed great artistic talent.

2. Confiscated my catapult for firing glacé

cherries at the window in cookery class.

3. Made me copy out the recipe for rock buns ten times for putting three tablespoons of pepper in the mixture.

4. Kept me in at break and made me sandpaper my desk for carving 'I heart J' on the lid with my compass. Worried because JT walked past and saw me doing it so I quickly turned the J into a fancy R in case he got any funny ideas and carved 'I heart Ross' which is what I meant to write. No idea why I put J.

5. Sent me out of class for giving Harry Dunn Blu-Tack in a sweet wrapper and pretending it was bubblegum.

Kenji says he's reporting me at the meeting on Monday because he wants to be a brain surgeon and can't concentrate with me messing about. Also his dad has promised him thousands of yuan if he gets into Oxford University. What a swot.

Hamster's going to report me for trying to choke her with a peppery rock bun but she shouldn't have been so greedy.

Mei Ling didn't say anything but is in cahoots with Kenji and kept giving me a ninja death stare so will prob. report me to the head of MI5 and Windy Hurricane at the school meeting.

So at least two people are going to report me – possibly three – YAY!

SATURDAY

Dear Diary,

Mousie has put herself back to bed + says she had headache, but I think it's because she didn't get any post . . . again.

I got a postcard from M & D and one from Kesi, and a packet of hollyhock seeds from G'ma which I asked her for. Pretended no one had sent me anything to spare Mousie's feelings. Will make big fuss of her on her b'day to make up for her useless parents. Not sure how yet, but I will think of something.

No one else to hang out with, so going to school garden, to see if JT's around. Might say sorry, might not. Depends on my mood.

SUNDAY

Dear Diary,

Gave hollyhock seeds to JT yesterday to say sorry. We planted them in pots together in the greenhouse. He's so easy to talk to and smells of peat + leaves + sunshine.

Don't fancy him though. Just as well because he doesn't fancy me either. Don't think he does anyway. Probably for the best. Be awful if he fell in love with me, because I'm leaving. Not that he ever would. Same as I'd never fall in love with him.

Pretty sure I'll be leaving after the meeting on Monday. Shauna had a right go at me this afternoon for spilling tiny bit of blackcurrant drink on my bedside rug. It was an *accident*. Carthorse did an impression of a camel giving birth and made me laugh and I squeezed the carton too hard and it squirted out of the straw.

It was only a few drops but Shauna said I'll have to pay for it to be dry-cleaned, so I emptied the rest of carton all over the rug till it went purple and she went nuts.

Have read my postcards from M & D and Kesi. Not much to report except this:

- Yellow baboons lick the night dew off their fur
- They make thirty different sounds including grunts, barks and screams (like Shauna)
- Bubba Tundi has his first tooth + is like Baby Jesus

- Mum has made friends with a dik-dik (an antelope, or so she says)
- G'ma lost her false teeth in the frozen section at Tesco and wants to know what I want for Christmas (it's only *spring* G'ma!)
- Everyone misses me + loves me + blah, blah, blah

Going to sort out Mousie's hair now because it's gone frizzy and she can't do the back by herself.

Mousie had an asthma attack earlier. Took her to see Matron in the sick bay and got a new refill for her puffer. She's OK but I don't want her to get stressed out. It makes her breathing worse so am giving her a make-over as well as a hairdo to take her mind off things.

Have borrowed Mei Ling's make-up bag while she's out spying or whatever it is she gets up to on the quiet. She doesn't know we're borrowing her stuff but she won't miss a bit of mascara, will she? Mousie's only got short eyelashes.

Mousie's Make-Over

Equipment:

Blusher
(shade: Cheeky Chops)

Glitter eyeshadow
(maybe it's
Maybelline, maybe
not – looks fake)

Hot rollers

Ladyshave

Mascara

Tweezers

Lipstick
(shade: Hot Chilli)

Heated eyelash
curlers

Method:

1. Wedge dorm door shut for privacy. Sit Mousie on chair, put hairband on and say, 'Relax, stop struggling. It'll be fun.'

2. Ask her which features she wants to enhance. Mousie's reply: 'This is pointless, Elizabeth. Get me a plastic surgeon.'

3. Decide what skin tone she is (white with orange dots).

4. Pluck eyebrows. Mousie says it's too painful and to use the Ladyshave which is a mistake because it mows half an eyebrow off. It's OK though because she snips some faux fur off her rabbit nightie case and we use it to re-turf the bald patch with Pritt Stick.

5. Put heated rollers in to smooth out frizz + put mascara on.

6. Try to get the mascara off as Mousie's eyes go all puffy. Think she's crying with joy because she looks so lush but turns

out she's allergic. Didn't know it's waterproof mascara. Can't find any remover so use some stuff we find in Carthorse's cabinet. Think it's baby oil but it's to lubricate her bike. It works though. At least Mousie stops squeaking.

7. Apply lipstick and blusher. Glitter eyeshadow compact explodes on opening and goes all over us like space dust so refill it with Sherbet Dip Dab so Mei Ling won't notice.

8. Remove rollers. Think the ones I used are a bit small because Mousie looks a demented poodle.

9. Wash her hair to get rid of poodle-curls, give her an updo with my scrunchy and you know what? Mousie says that after her make-over, she really appreciates how she looks naturally and laughs like she means it.

10. Told her she's beautiful.

MONDAY

Dear Diary,

I hate Blightleafe. I HATE IT. Can't stand it a second longer.

Have just run out of the stupid school meeting. I'm so angry, I'm crying.

How dare the jury disrespect M & D and say they haven't brought me up properly – they have! They are the best parents ever. It's not their fault I misbehave! You *know* the reason!

It started off OK. When Windy asked if anyone needed money for anything, John T. said he'd like a new spade because the handle fell off his. Mr Johns backed him up, so they gave John £15 and I was v happy for him. Then they handed out the pocket money. Thought I wasn't going to get any, but I did. Got a tenner so thought that's OK then, at least I can get Mousie a b'day present.

Then Rebekah asked if anyone had any complaints and I thought, *Oh, here we go. It'll be all about me.* But instead, a kid in our class called Humphrey Pickleton grassed up Harry Dunn for cheating in maths. Windy Hurricane made out like it's the crime of century and people were calling for Harry to be beheaded/hung, drawn and quartered etc. but Rebekah went all girl-power with Windy's hammer and said the punishment has to fit the crime. Harry was in bits and said he only copied Grumphrey's answers because he's struggling with algebra + his dad gets angry if he gets anything less than C+. Me + Mousie felt really sorry for him ☹.

Think Rebekah did too – she asked Mr Johns if he'd give Harry extra help with maths and he said yes. But Harry still has to sit by himself for a week so he's not tempted to cheat again.

Then the poop hit the fan. Windy asked if anyone had any other complaints and Shauna said, 'I have serious complaints to make about

Elizabeth Allen,' and got a flimmin' list out!

Won't tell you the whole list because it's too long – I'm always rude, always interrupting, go to bed late, blah, blah, blah, but then she told them about the blackcurrant juice on rug incident and Rebekah said, 'We'll send it to the cleaners and Elizabeth will have to pay for it.'

Next – can you believe this? Maurice the monitor marched over and TOOK MY TENNER OFF ME! How can I buy Mousie a present now?

Then Windy changed my bedtime to 7.30 instead of 8 p.m. for being late so often. So now I'll miss Mr Lewis's concerts + the school dance. When I objected v loudly, Rebekah said she'll change it back next week if I'm sensible – like *that's* going to happen!

Thought it was all done and dusted, but Windy wouldn't shut up. He said, 'About Elizabeth's rudeness. I'm not sure she can help herself. Usually, children with behavioural problems have never been taught any manners, so her parents are to blame.'

I don't care if he is Head Boy. No one disrespects my mum and dad. Was so angry I shrieked at him right in front of the teachers.

'HOW DARE YOU! TAKE THAT BACK! MY M & D ARE BETTER THAN YOURS, YOU SON OF A BABOON!'

Windy said, 'Thanks, Elizabeth. You've just proved my point.'

But it *still* wasn't over.

When Rebekah asked if there were any more complaints, Kenji started bleating on about me 'spoiling lessons' and can the jury do something to stop me or he'll never get to go to Oxford. Miss Ranger nodded so violently her glasses fell off.

Rebekah looked v shocked and said, 'I didn't know Elizabeth was *that* bad – has nobody got a good word to say about her?'

Seemed NOT. But then of all people, dear shy

Mousie stood up, all stammery and blushing and said: 'I-I-I should like to speak up for Elizabeth. She has been a g-good friend to me and isn't nearly as bad as she pretends.'

I could have hugged her. Will do later. So brave of her, sticking up for me like that. I said, 'There! Stick that in your pipe and smoke it, Windy.'

But he said Mousie saying nice things about me wasn't enough. He asked what my favourite lessons are and the idiots in my class yelled, 'Riding, music and art.'

Now he's banned me from those lessons for a whole week. And I'm not allowed to go to the village.

Kicked my chair over and ran out. Now I'm lying on my bed and I've run out of tissues + got *snot* down my tie + wish I'd never been *born* and I can't . . . stop . . . CRY . . . ING!

Dear Diary,

Mousie just came looking for me and caught me booing. Felt pathetic as I'm meant to be the tough one. She didn't make a big thing of it though. Just gave me a squeeze, told me to splash my face with cold water and meet her in the common room. She wanted to play tennis but it's raining so we'll play ping pong indoors.

Thanked Mousie for sticking up for me but asked her not to do it again, as even though my punishments are total bumsville and Windy dissed my parents, at least I'm closer to getting kicked out.

But she said, 'Are you sure? No one's ever been expelled from Whyteleafe, not even for letting Windy's tyres down.'

I never knew that. I said, 'I'm *trapped*, Mousie. What do I have to do to get out of here – commit homicide?'

115

What Mousie Said:

I really, really don't want you to go BUT . . .

I want you to be happy + reunited with Ross + Saus + Beans.

The problem is, there are lots of reasons why you can't run away:

1. You have no train fare.
2. Your house is locked up.
3. Uncle Ru has one bedroom flat + Sebastian sleeps on sofa bed.
4. If you stay with G'ma she will make you watch *Coronation Street* + drown you in cups of tea.

But you could go and see Rebekah and say: 'I will behave BEAUTIFULLY from now on if you please ask Miss Beast + Beauty to ring my M & D and tell them to take me out of Whyteleafe at half-term because I'm so unhappy + stressed and my education is suffering.'

This is a genius plan! If it works – which it might – I stand a *far* better chance of being sent home if I'm good because I've asked nicely! That's great because, actually, being bad all the time is hard work. And I will get to hang out with Mousie + JT for bit longer. Not that I fancy him but I'd like to see the hollyhocks sprout.

I said, 'Thanks, Mousie. You're the best!'

And she said, 'No need to thank me, Monkey. That's what friends are for.'

I hooted and said, 'You just called me Monkey – why?'

And she said, 'Well, you like baboons and primates and you call me Mousie.'

I asked if she minds me calling her that. 'Be honest,' I said. 'I'll call you Joanna if you want. Or Jo. How about Jo?' But she said she doesn't like the others calling her Mousie, but she knows I mean it in a good way and not to stop because she likes it. So now we are Mousie and Monkey ☺☺. We've truly bonded.

Tuesday

Dear Diary,

Everyone went riding today but I couldn't go because of Windy's punishment regime. But did I make a fuss? NO!

I stayed with Miss Ranger, got on with my geography project and impressed her greatly with my neat map of Africa + huge knowledge of baboons.

She said, 'Goodness. I never knew baboons caught flu, Elizabeth. That's absolutely fascinating.'

She suggested I stuck in my postcards of hyenas from M & D and Kesi to add some colour. She even gave me some see-through sticky-backed corners so I didn't spoil them with glue. My project looks really good now. Miss Ranger says if I carry on working hard like this she'll give me an A. Was gutted I had to miss my music lesson though. I thought Mr Lewis was going to cry when I told him why.

He said, 'Oh, you silly little personage! I've asked Ricardo Marconi in Year 10 to learn the duet from *The Rocky Horror Show*. I wanted you two to play it together. You are my only pupil who is up to his standard. What a shame.'

SHAME? It's worse than that! Ricardo Marconi is only the coolest guy in the whole school. Mei Ling reckons his dad's in the Mafia. His mum's from Cleethorpes. Even so, he's seriously hot. Not a patch on JT though. Not that JT's hot, but he's got a warm personality.

Sorry, got distracted there, Diary. But listen, Ricardo is the best pianist. You should hear him in assembly. He's like a pro.

I'm so flattered Mr Lewis thinks I'm good enough to duet with him. But now I can't as am banned from music for a whole week. So I begged. 'Could you teach me the duet *next* week, sir?

Please, sir! I have to do this. I'll be good all week, I promise. Then Windy – I mean William Murricane – will let me go to music class.'

Love Mr Lewis. He gets me. He could see I was losing it, so he patted my shoulder (awww), gave me the duet music and said to practise it by myself. Then next week he'll ask Ricardo along and we can have a go at it together . . . yay!

Dear Diary,

It's 7.30 p.m. On my own, tucked up in bed like a toddler. Nearly didn't stick to 7.30 rule as I wanted to practise the duet. Told Mousie I was going up at 8 p.m. like normal and would pretend my watch was slow to Shauna but she said, 'Don't risk it, Monkey. Remember the plan.'

Shauna was very surprised to catch me in PJs under my duvet. She looked a bit smug for a sec but then asked if we could talk.

I panicked because she sat on my bed and

looked at me with her head on one side like she had bad news. Terrible things went through my mind:

- Dad's been trampled by a herd of wildebeest
- Sausage has gone missing + Beans is suicidal
- G'ma has hit a pedestrian with her mobility scooter again

But it wasn't any of that. Shauna was just in shock cos I'd done as she'd asked and thought I must be ill. I said, 'I'm fine apart from blackheads.'

And she said, 'Ah, great. It's a drag having to go to bed early but well done you for sticking to the rules.'

Then she gave me her *Cosmopolitan* mag to read and said I can keep the free nail polish, like she's my big sister or something.

'The jury hates punishing you like this,' she

said. 'I feel for you, I do. I was a hooligan when I first came here. I was so gobby, they took my pocket money off me for a whole month + banned me from everything except eating + breathing + peeing. But I realised I'd have a much better craic if I fell into line and, you know what, Elizabeth? I've had a ball. They even made me a monitor – me! There's hope for you yet. Just keep your head down. By the next meeting, you'll be laughing.'

Then she rolled up the blackcurranty rug and said she'll take it to cleaners for me. I like her much more now I know she's a reformed hooligan. And she's got rid of her moustache.

Wednesday

Dear Diary,

Fed up because I wasn't allowed to go on the sketching trip this morning but had a good laugh with Mousie at break after French. Don't know why but I find speaking *en français* quite easy, so even if I muck about, I don't get behind. I had a private French tutor but she got pregnant and had twins so she wouldn't have to teach me. I didn't mess around today though. The plan to be on my best behaviour and all that. What I did instead was stand on my chair and sing the song M'selle asked us to learn.

M'selle said my performance of 'Non, Je Ne Regrette Rien' was *'formidable'* and *'magnifique'* and *'encore, s'il vous plaît!'* So I sang it again with big arm movements, like a diva, and everyone clapped. I was word-perfect, pitch-perfect and modest. I regret nothing. But Mousie does. She's v bright – much better at maths than me – but French is not her strong point. *Elle est très terrible.* She went scarlet when it was her turn to sing and got stage fright + forgot the words + regretted every second.

After the bell, M'selle steered me into the stationery cupboard and asked me to ' 'Elp poor leetle Zho-anna learn ze song. Always she makes ze mistakes.'

I said, '*Mais oui. Ce n'est pas un problème,* M'selle.'

And she said, '*Merci beaucoup,* Elizabet. No matter what ze ozzer's zay, I sink you 'ave ze very beeg 'eart.'

Not sure why Whyteleafe employs a French teacher

who can't master the English accent but she sounds quite cute, *non*?

Told Mousie I was going to help her with her French song and she said, '*Mon dieu! Non!*' because she was worried the boys might hear her + laugh etc., so we went in the girls' loo. I sang a line, then Mousie copied it, I sang it again etc. and she soon got the hang of it. We had such a laugh because we didn't know Carthorse + Smellie Marsden were in other cubicles and they suddenly joined in with our song while they were having a wee. Then we formed a quartet in front of the sinks and Carthorse conducted us with a bog brush.

We made so much noise, Miss Beast came clumping in wearing her Dr Martens and said, 'What are you doing, ladies?'

We said, 'M'selle asked us to practise.'

And she said, 'V good but put that lavatory brush back where it belongs please, Melinda Carter. And wash your hands, dear.'

Je suis très heureuse.

THURSDAY

Dear Diary,

Mousie went to the village this afternoon and v kindly brought me back a Snickers bar and a Solero ice lolly because I'm banned from going, remember?

She didn't have anyone to go with, so I had a word in Carthorse's earhole and she said fine, she'd go with Mousie because she needed to buy deodorant. Hers isn't working because she sweats like a beast so I said to try a stronger brand called Mitchum, which I read about in Shauna's *Cosmopolitan*, and gave her the money-off coupon + a glimpse of the problem page that had a letter about flatulence + farting which I thought might help her too.

While Mousie was gone, I practised the duet in the school hall. It's not easy because it's actually a Grade 5 piece. Mr Lewis swung by just as I hit a bum note but he just said, 'Don't mind me. You're doing fine. Keep it up.'

When Mousie came back, we went to the school garden to admire JT's new spade. On the way, a gang of boys from Year 3 started yelling, 'Oh look! It's Elizabeth the Worst and her pet rat.'

I rushed at them but Mousie held me back and said, 'Ignore them, Monkey. They're just trying to wind you up so you get punished.'

Wanted to slap them for calling Mousie a rat but she said she's been called worse + doesn't want me to get into trouble over a silly thing like that and to forget about it. So I walked away.

JT was digging a hole with his new spade when we found him. I asked him what he was planting and he said, 'Harry's pet goldfish.' Apparently poor old Sandy went belly-up in his tank last night and Harry was too upset to bury him so John said he would.

I said we ought to give Sandy a proper funeral because Harry really loved that fish. JT agreed so I wrapped poor deceased fishy in Mousie's hanky, made a cross to mark his grave out of my lolly stick and wrote 'R.I.P. Sandy Dunn. Best fish ever' on it.

John dug up a marigold that had self-seeded in his radish patch and planted it on the grave. Mousie said we should sing some fishy hymns so we sang 'For Those in Peril on the Sea' and 'One, Two, Three, Four, Five, Once I Caught a Fish Alive' and 'When You Fish Upon a Star'.

Glad we gave Sandy a nice send-off. Hopefully it will give Harry comfort when we tell him about it. He can visit the grave whenever he likes, John said. Such a lovely thing to say, I went all wobbly inside. Probably just coming down with a bug.

FRIDAY

Dear Diary,

Got another letter from M & D + photo of Bubba Tundi from Kesi. Don't know what she's feeding Bubba on but he's HUGE. He looks so juicy. Hope the baboons don't steal him – they do that sometimes. He's probably too heavy for them to lift though.

Mum sent me stamps – 12 x 1st class + 12 x 2nd class – so I gave half to Mousie. She spends all her money on stamps. She was v pleased but got sad again cos it's so one way, her sending all those letters to her M & D and never getting any back.

She's started worrying about her b'day again. It's not far off now and when I gave her the stamps, she said if her mum sends her a b'day cake, she'll give me half to say thank you.

But she knows I know that's not gonna happen, which made it even worse. Everyone should have a b'day cake. It's the law. Will do something about this or my name's not Elizabeth A.

SATURDAY

Dear Diary,

Weekend. Woo-hoo. No lessons. Really sunny. Weather too nice to stay in and practise duet so will do it before bed.

Mei Ling went off this morning wearing aviator sunglasses. Probably on a spy mission, incognito.

Smellie Marsden and Carthorse went for a

paddle in the Mill Pond. Noticed Carthorse forgot her swimming cozzie which means she went skinny-dipping in the nuddy. Hope she didn't startle the cows. Or the farmer. Will ask.

Mousie threw up after lunch so I took her to Matron and she told her to have a lie-down in the sick bay so she could keep an eye on her.

Hamster was busy on her hamster wheel or similar so I helped JT in garden all day. We got loads done. Did masses of weeding, dug a new flower bed + laid slabs to make path. He said, 'You're a lot stronger than you look, Bizzy Lizzy.' Don't know why that made my heart sing tra la but it did. My back was killing me but I didn't tell him that in case he thinks I'm a weed instead of a beautiful hardy bedding plant. So hot, he took his T-shirt off. Nice abs. Not that I was looking. I was wearing my athletics vest and he touched my shoulder and went, 'Tsss! You're burning.' Oh and I was burning. I was!

Went to say goodnight to Mousie in the sick

bay earlier and she said, 'You look really happy, Monkey. What have you been up to?'

I said, 'Gardening.'

And she said, 'Are you blushing?'

And I said, 'No, I caught the sun.'

And she smiled and said, 'You love it at Whyteleafe now, don't you? Admit it, you don't want to leave.'

'I do want to leave,' I said. 'Don't be fooled, Mousie. I'm just trying to make the most of it till I can get out of this dump, OK?'

She threw her hands in the air, said, 'Whatever,' then she turned her back on me. That took the smile right off my face.

SUNDAY

Dear Diary,

Glad to report Mousie is much better. Matron thinks she might have an intolerance to nuts – or was it nutters? In which case I fear for Mousie's health as this place is full of them.

Weather still hot so am taking Mousie to see what JT and I did to the garden yesterday, then having a picnic on the school field with my dormies. Shauna can't come because she's going 'birdwatching' with a boy from Year 10. She said it's not a date but she was wearing a dress and no binoculars so we don't believe her.

Smellie and Carthorse went to the farmers' market in the village to buy the food and everyone chipped in. I said I wouldn't eat anything cos I couldn't pay my own way, but Smellie said she'd pay for me and I can pay her back whenever as long as I stop calling her Smellie, so I said OK because she was being nice to me.

Anyway, by the time they got to the village, the market had shut apart from the bread stall + French stall so they had to go to the corner shop to pad out the picnic a bit.

What We Had on Our Picnic:

- Pork scratchings
- Rustic bread filled with cheese strings
- Avocado with salad cream and Quavers
- Chocolate Flake sarnies
- French crepe with ham, egg and Twiglets
- Bison pate
- Packet Mr Kipling jam tarts
- Packet Viennese whirls
- Tin of baby mandarins
- Fanta
- Diet Coke

Best meal ever.

MONDAY

Dear Diary,

Am in the gym. Have left the school meeting while they discuss what to do with me. The jury haven't come across a case like mine before, so now Miss Beauty + Miss Beast have got involved.

Had great reports from Shauna + Miss Ranger + M'selle so I got pocket money this week. As am in everyone's best books, I also asked for money to buy Mr Lewis's sea piece and unbelievably Windy said yes, because I deserve a reward for being so good.

He even took back what he said about M & D being rubbish parents because I'd shown that I know how to behave last week.

BUT – then I landed my bombshell on Rebekah about leaving at half-term. I said exactly what Mousie told me to say re. our plan, i.e.

I knew they wouldn't send me home if I was bad, so I've been really good so could they please, please call M & D and tell them to take me out of here because I hate it and they wouldn't want me to be unhappy.

Miss Beast asked if I'd like to leave the room while they discuss me because it's not very nice to sit and listen to what people think. I said I'll be really bad again if they make wrong decision and Mousie went, 'Eek!'

Miss Beauty said, 'Don't say anything else, Elizabeth, my dear. Off you trot. We'll call you back when we've decided what to do for the best.'

They are taking ages. Can't stand this. Am going to the school hall to practise the duet to take my mind off it. Bet they make me stay. If they do, I'll run away and sleep rough in woods if Uncle Ru won't have me.

Dear Diary,

Mousie just came running into the hall all out of puff and said she thought I'd gone to the gym and had been looking for me everywhere. Told her if I ever go missing, I'll either be on the piano, hiding in the woods, or at Uncle Ru's. Or the greenhouse.

'The plan worked!'

I said, '*WHAT?!* You are joking, aren't you?'

And Mousie said, 'No. Am I laughing? I'm telling you the truth.'

Then she told me what they said:

1. Some of the kids said to get rid of me now (e.g. Humphrey) because I'm a pain and they don't want me here.

2. Mousie stuck up for me in front of the whole school and said, 'You *would* want her here if you knew her like I do. Monkey is kind, generous, funny, clever and wonderful. But she wants to go home

and, even though I want her to stay, that's selfish if she's sad.' So . . .

3. Miss Beast said I can go at half-term if I'm really unhappy and can HONESTLY say so at the meeting.

4. Miss Beauty said if everyone helps me to have a happy time at Whyteleafe, hopefully I'll choose to stay of my own free will.

5. Everyone stamped their feet + clapped at this cunning plan except Humphrey.

Going back to the meeting now to be told what's happening even though I already know.

Dear Diary,

Thought the meeting was going to be really awkward but Rebekah just said, 'Promise to be as good as we know you can be till half-term, then if you still *genuinely* want to go home, Miss

Best + Miss Belle will call your mum + dad and you can leave. We want you to stay though.'

I was so choked up with all the love in the air, I promised in front of the whole school. Windy said, 'Good for you,' and lifted my punishments. So now I can go to bed at 8 p.m. again + go riding, painting + piano-ing etc. Yee-ha! Best of both worlds:

- I get to stay with Mousie a bit longer
- I get to play the duet with Ricardo
- I get to stuff it up M & D by showing them I was right, they were wrong and they can't send me away

Off to the village with Mousie after lunch to buy sea music and our celebration feast: two cans Lilt, Kinder Eggs, Munchies, Flumps.

Tuesday

Dear Diary,

Got my sea music and some lettuce seeds yesterday. Said I'll give Mousie the first lettuce when it grows but she said it will only be as big as a Brussels sprout if I leave at half-term. Gave her permish to pick it in my absence when it's big enough and said I'll tell JT to make extra sure the slugs don't eat it. He hates putting pellets down because he's eco-friendly, so we use crushed egg shells because slugs hate getting them on their slimy bits and go away.

G'ma sent me a chocolate cake the size of a tractor wheel. Shared it with everyone and Shauna said, 'Great cake! Jeebus, you've changed Elizabeth, so you have! Remember when you first came and wouldn't let anyone have single crumb?' Arghh – don't remind me what a selfish moo I was. Maybe if Kesi knew how lovely I am now, she'd come back to live with us and bring Tundi. He could be my step-bubba.

love from Grandma x

Dear Diary,

Went to music lesson with Mr Lewis this afternoon. Ricardo Marconi was there! Didn't realise we were duetting today. I was all ☺ but Ricardo just looked at me like I was poo on his shoe and said, 'Sir, do I have to play it with her? She's a *girl*.'

Mr Lewis ignored that sexist remark and just said, 'When you're ready, Mr Marconi,' and gave me the bass part and him the treble. He counted us in and I played pretty flimmin' well and although Ricardo is right up himself, we made beautiful music together. Mr Lewis said, 'See, Ricardo? I've found you the perfect partner.' But he just tutted like G'ma, which was rude.

Mr Lewis grinned at me like he thought Ricardo was being a total loser and told him to come back later for his lesson, and to make sure he practises with me in his spare time.

By the look on Ricardo's face, you'd think Mr

Lewis had asked him to snog a warthog. So I snapped, 'Play with someone else then! You think you're so clever but I played way better than you did and you know it. You hit three bum notes – didn't he, sir!'

Then Ricardo piped up: 'She hit *four*, sir.'

Mr Lewis balanced his violin bow on his upper lip like a moustache to get our attention and said he understands creative temperament and 'all that jazz' (and he did jazz hands) but if Ricardo refuses to play nicely, he can do the duet with Harry Dunn instead.

That knocked him right off his high horse. He said, 'I'll play with Allen, sir. Dunn's fingers are like a bunch of bananas.'

Hooted my head off about the banana fingers. Could tell Ricardo liked me laughing at his description because he grinned at me and said, 'OK, you not-a so rarr-bbish. I will practise with you, *bimba*,' in a dodgy Italian accent, then with a 'Ciao,' he strutted off, combing his hair into a huge bouffey shape.

When he had gone, Mr Lewis played the duet with me and pointed out my four bummers. I used to hate it when my private tutors pointed out my mistakes but I don't mind when he does it. Told him I'd bought the sea music. He was chuffed as nuts and said he'll teach me how to play it so I can perform it at the end of term concert. Yay.

Then I remembered I won't be here. Told him I'm leaving at half-term because they said I could if I'm unhappy. 'And are you unhappy?' he asked. 'Are any of us truly happy?'

I said, 'I don't know, sir,' and he started banging his head on the piano and swearing and said to forget learning the sea music – he'll teach it to someone who wants to stay.

I said, 'Fine, I'll learn it all by myself then!'

He said, 'Why bother?'

And I said, 'Because I LOVE it, sir. It makes me so HAPPY.'

Mr Lewis said that was all he wanted to hear and that he'll teach it to me whether I stay or leave because . . .

'Your appreciation of MacDowell's 'Opus 55' is truly refreshing, Elizabeth, and frankly none of my other pupils give a ferret's fart.'

So lyrical.

Wednesday

Dear Diary,

I've screwed up. Done something disgustingly mean cos Harry Dunn was really winding me up when I sat next to JT at breakfast.

He started singing at the top of his voice: 'Elizabeth and JT sitting in a tree, K-I-S-S-I-N-G,' (which we were *not*! Not in a tree) and John got v embarrassed and walked out.

Everyone was going, 'Oooh. Elizabeth loves John,' and giggling. I was so furious I had to get my own back on Dunn.

When he went to get his third lot of bacon, I saw he'd left his blazer on his chair, so I filled his pockets with porridge.

Mousie said, 'No, Monkey, don't!' because when Harry found out who did it, he'd get me back. I didn't care. He had it coming.

He didn't notice the porridge till art class when he put his hands in his pockets to find his hanky. He looked like he had porridge gloves on. I giggled and he glared at me so I mouthed, 'Yeah. What are you going to do about it, Dunn?' and he pulled a face.

Thought he'd blab to Miss Ranger, but no. He just washed his hands and sat down again, so I thought he'd let it go and carried on painting my picture of Ross. But when I went to wash my paintbrush, everyone started nudging each other and laughing.

I said, 'What's so funny?'

They said, 'Noth-ing, Elizabeth!' *Giggle-giggle-splutter.*

Mousie wasn't in class because she had a migraine or she'd have told me what they were all wetting themselves about. So I never found out till break. Went across the playground to find her, and Harry Dunn and his boy mates were all following me and pointing and saying, 'Is it true? Ugh! Poor him!'

I turned round and said, 'What are you losers going on about?' and told them to shut up or I'd slap them. Then I heard Mousie calling, so I ran over to her.

She told me to turn around and then said, 'Someone's stuck a notice on your back.'

I ♥ JOHN TERRY!

She took it off and showed me. It said, and I'm going bright red and sweaty telling you this:

I heart John Terry. Mousie said, 'Let it go, Monkey. It's not worth it.'

No way. I chased after Harry Dunn, waved the notice in his face and screamed, 'Did you write this?'

He said, 'Yes, babe. Payback for the porridge gloves.'

I tore it up in his face and said, 'How *dare* you!' and 'I am *not* your babe.'

And he said, 'Ugh . . . no! You're *John's*.'

That did it. I slapped him right round the chops and called him a lying, cheating, pigging cheat.

Everyone gathered round, chanting, 'Fight! Fight!' Then Shauna came barging over and asked what the jeebus was going on.

Humphrey grassed me up and said I slapped Harry + called him a cheat and Shauna told me to say sorry. Why should I? He started it. So I said, 'No, I'm not saying sorry to that piggin' liar and cheat – he should say sorry to *me*! Report him at the next meeting!'

I went to kick him and my shoe flew off, so Shauna said, 'Icy calm, Elizabeth. Come and tell Auntie Shauna all about it,' and frogmarched me off to the common room.

I was glad it was empty because I was really upset – with myself for losing it and with Harry for what he wrote. I will never be able to look JT in the eye again. Shauna gave me a tissue, put the torn-up note back together on the ping pong table and read it. I was cringing but she said, 'Aww. That's quite sweet, isn't it?'

SWEET? I've never been so humiliated and it's not even true!

Shauna said, 'Fair do's, Elizabeth. Even if it *was* true, you don't want your love life shouted all around town, do you now? Unless you're Ellie Marsden. Why did Harry pick on you, I wonder?'

I told her about the porridge and she laughed and said, 'Ah, come on, did you really expect him to take that lying down? If you play pranks on him, you have to expect a bit of tit for tat.'

I still want her to report him at the meeting but Shauna said she never reports pranks. I said *I'll* report him then and she said, 'That's telling tales. You don't want to be a snitch. Don't go spoiling this good week of yours over a silly thing like this.'

She said she should report *me* for saying Harry's a cheat cos he's already been punished for that. He's mended his ways and is really ashamed he'd cheated, then I reminded everybody, which was really mean, so it was.

Wish I hadn't called Harry names now. He deserved a slap but he didn't deserve me calling him what I did. I'm actually disgusted with myself. Everyone will think I'm cruel and evil and I've broken my promise to Miss Beauty &

Miss Beast. I bet they won't let me go home now.

Felt really weepy but Shauna said, 'Ah, come on. It's not that bad. Say sorry to Harry and I won't report you, OK?'

Like *that's* going to work. But she said it might because Harry's a sweet softy. She's right. He cried over Sandy's grave and I never teased him or told anyone because I felt sorry for him. I know what it's like to lose someone you love.

But I hate saying sorry. Shauna said a little thing like saying sorry can make all the difference but I'm not sure. Mousie thinks I should say sorry too. Even though she's on my side and knows how I feel about JT. What to do?

Will sleep on it.

THURSDAY

Dear Diary,

I said sorry to Harry. He was with all his mates. I wanted to say it in private but he said if I had something to say, to spit it out.

So I said, 'I'm really sorry for slapping you and for calling you those names.'

He looked a bit ☹ then ☺ and said, 'Oh, OK. Forget it. I'm sorry about the note. Shake hands?'

I held my hand out and he thumbed his nose and my heart sank, thinking he hadn't really forgiven me at all, but he was only messing. He gave me a bear hug and lifted me right up off the ground and whispered in my ear, 'Thanks for not telling my mates I blubbed over Sandy. Want a baby rabbit?'

Ohhhh. Baby rabbits! *Baby* rabbits! Mwa, mwa, wa!

Saying sorry was *that* easy. So glad I listened to Shauna's and Mousie's advice. Harry said he's got an old hutch I can have when the babies are old enough to leave their mum – after half-term. Oh no! I really want one of Harry's babies – well, not HIS babies – a baby *rabbit*. But I can't. Won't be here much longer. I told him and he said, 'You're not still banging on about leaving, are you?'

I am still banging on actually. But baby rabbits are so cute . . .

FRIDAY

Dear Diary,

I really want a baby rabbit.

SATURDAY

Dear Diary,

Still want a baby rabbit. The fluffy ginger one with white paws and ears. Going to give it a cuddle.

SUNDAY

Dear Diary,

Did I mention I want a baby rabbit? I'm going to kiss it + stroke it and call it Jonty. Going to the school garden now. Hopefully JT has forgotten Porridge Gate. The lettuce seedlings need thinning. And the carrots. Busy, busy.

M⊚NDAY

Dear Diary,

Went to the school meeting. No one had anything bad to say about me (I thanked Shauna for keeping her trap shut about Harry). Got my pocket money but OH CRUD forgot to ask for extra money to give Mousie a b'day she'll never forget. Bummer. Really need that money as I have a plan up my sleeve.

Seen a really nice red handbag in the shoe shop in the village. Don't think it's leather because it's £9.99 in the sale but I know she'll love it. Got enough money to buy it but need more cos I want to get her lots of things because her mum and dad won't. Could club together with the other girls but I want it to be from me and choose stuff I know Mousie likes. Could put tights over my head and rob a bank. Bit risky though and Uncle Ru says prison food sucks.

Tuesday

Dear Diary,

I got post! There is a god! Uncle Ru sent me £50! He said it's to make up for not getting me a Crimbo present – he forgot because Sebastian slipped a disc playing Widow Twankey in the panto and he had to nurse him 24/7.

£50! I'm going to give Mousie the best b'day ever. And here's the ta da! I'm going to say the handbag + lip gloss are from me but pretend all the rest is from her *mum*. It will make her feel so loved!

Plan for Mousie's Birthday:

Budget:

£60 (This week's pocket money + Uncle Ru's dosh.)

Shopping List:

Red handbag (£9.99)
Cherry lip gloss (£2)
Wildlife book by David Attenborough
   (reduced to £5.99)
Sparkly b'day card (£2.50)
Another b'day card (£1.99)
Massive cake with candles (£35-40?)
Wrapping paper (£2)

Wednesday

Dear Diary,

I have a *problemo* as Ricardo Marconi would say. Going to the village at lunchtime to buy gifts + order b'day cake but can't go with Mousie because it's all for her. Will ask Carthorse to drag her off to Trampoline Club. Let's hope they don't do doubles and jump at the same time or the Carthorse will boing Mousie into orbit.

Couldn't concentrate in French. M'selle asked me a question but I wasn't listening and she said, '*Zut alors*! What eez wrong wiz you ziz morning, Elizabet?' and said she'd keep me behind after class if I didn't pull my '*petite chaussettes*' up.

Found Ellie in the bogs and asked if she'll come to the village with me. She said yes and asked what I wanted to buy so I pretended it's something v embarrassing and told her she'll have to sit in the café and promise not to look in my bags. She kept trying to guess and said, 'Is it spot cream? Is it bum cream? Is it panty liners?' like we were playing 20 Questions.

Meeting her at school gates in a min. Got my purse.

Dear Diary,

Just got back from village. Have secretly ordered ginormous b'day cake with sugar flowers + fresh cream + eleven candles. Asked baker to write 'Happy birthday to our darling Joanna' in swirly icing on top, so Mousie thinks it's from her M & D.

Saw Shauna gawping at me through baker's window so had to pretend I'd just bought Eccles cakes for me + Ellie.

It cost extra to have the b'day cake delivered so I was worried I wouldn't be able to afford the Attenborough book. Luckily I got the shopkeeper to reduce it even more as it has a slightly damaged cover. (Which might have been me but it's for a good cause ☺.)

Bought everything on my list + nice wrapping paper with butterflies on. Was imagining Mousie's happy face when she saw cake + opened gift and feeling really good about it all when Ellie looked at my shopping bags and said, 'Wow. You got a lot of stuff for a tenner. Is it all from the chemist? That's one hell of a disease.'

OH BUM! Forgotten I'm meant to put all my money in box at the next meeting. Just blown Uncle Ru's entire £50!

Didn't fess up to Ellie because she can't keep a secret. Didn't mean to break the rules. What's done is done.

Thought I'd got away with it but after I'd hid all my shopping under my bed, Shauna came storming into the dorm demanding to know where I got the £50 note from she saw me waving in the baker's and said, 'I wasn't born yesterday. Eccle cake, my backside.'

I'd been sussed, so no point lying to her. Told her Uncle Ru sent it. When she asked why I hadn't saved it to put in the box, I said I genuinely forgot and spent it all.

She said, 'Jeebus, the whole fifty pounds? What on?'

I said, 'Please don't ask – it's a secret. I didn't spend it on me.'

But she said I've broken the rules and if I refuse to tell her, I can tell the whole meeting and Windy can deal with me. Thought she was my mate and would let me get away with it but she keeps switching. The power's gone to her head.

Lose-lose situation. I'm stuffed. Just as well Mousie's b'day is before the meeting or the jury would ruin it. Will just have to take what's coming to me after that.

THURSDAY

Dear Diary,

Mousie's b'day tomoz! Woke at 5.30 a.m. and wrote her cards under my duvet – one in my handwriting + one mum-stylee.

Also wrote a dedication in the Attenborough book mum-stylee and wrapped it in brown paper I found in the art cupboard.

Put a 1st class stamp on the 'From Mum' card + four 1st class stamps on the 'From Mum' book (v heavy, no time to weigh it). Addressed both to: Joanna Townsend, Whyteleafe School, Frampshire etc.

Bunged them in the letterbox early so they'll get here tomorrow. Will grab the 'Mum' card and prezzie when they arrive and scribble on the postmarks so Mousie can't read them, *then* give them to her. Otherwise she might see they were posted from here, not her mum's house + break her heart. That's not happening.

Message in My Card:

To my BF Mousie,
Happy birthday x billion-trillion-zillion!
Hope this is your best birthday ever.
Loads of love, Monkey xxxxxxxxxxxxxxxxxxxxxxx

Message in 'Mum' Card:

To our darling daughter, Joanna,
Wishing you every happiness on your 11th birthday.
You are always in our hearts.
With all our love, Mum and Dad xxxxxxx

Will wrap + label Mousie's prezzies from me when she's asleep tonight.

FRIDAY

Dear Diary,

Woo-hoo. Mousie's b'day! Just nipped down to check post in my PJs. Gift and letter from Mousie's 'mum' arrived! Dealt with postmarks and put them back in Mousie's pigeonhole. Am back in bed pretending I've just woken up. Am so excited for Mousie + can't wait to see the big smile on her little freckly mush. Will wake her up now and wish her happy b'day.

Dear Diary,

Nooooo! It's all going wrong. Mousie's run off and locked herself in the loo. Think she's crying. I so wanted everything to be perfect. She woke up really sad so I tried to jolly her up, saying, 'Wonder how many cards you'll get, Mousie?' and, 'Bet you'll get a cake!'

Then Ellie spoilt the mood by saying, 'Why would she get anything? She's never has before,' like Mousie's deaf.

Carthorse said, 'I'd have got you a card, Jo, but I didn't know it was your birthday.' Hamster had completely forgotten and pretended to be asleep. Mei Ling said she never sends cards because it means cutting down the rainforest but hopes Mousie 'has a fun day'.

All the joy I tried to spread was going right down the pan so I sang 'Happy b'day to You!' and pogoed up and down on Mousie's bed to see if that would help but she put her hands over her ears and said, 'Will you all just *shut up* about my birthday!' and ran off.

But she is not pooping out of her special day – shan't let her if it's the last thing I do. The others have gone to breakfast so when she comes out of toilet, I will give her my gift + card.

Dear Diary,

Mousie still in loo. Maybe sad + constipated? Bad b'day combo. Forgot to say that when I got up early, I bumped into Harry and blagged a baby bunny off him for Mousie. It has to live with its mum for a bit longer but he's bringing it to show her after breakfast. Bit jealous – wish it was my bunny but we can share him.

Dear Diary,

Yay! Ambushed Mousie and gave her my gifts. She LOVES the red handbag + lip gloss. She said they are the best presents ever and hugged me so hard I thought I might get a collapsed lung.

Went with her to letter rack and when she saw the card + present with her name on, she looked really shocked and got her puffer out. Then she opened them and squealed + jumped up and down + kept saying, 'They remembered my *birthday*! Look, Monkey! I got a lovely big card to our darling Joanna *and* a book – look at this book, Monkey. It's by *Attenborough* – my hero!'

I said, 'Wow!' and, 'Brilliant!' and, 'See? They do love you, Mousie!'

She took the prezzies to the dining room to show everyone and there was a WHOPPING GREAT cardboard box on her chair. I said, 'Ung? I wonder who that's from. Open it quickly!'

Mousie was scared to in case it was a prank but everyone was saying, 'Open it! Open it!' so she did and gasped:

'OHHH MY DAYS! Look what Mum's sent me! It's got my name on in icing and flowers + candles + everything – it's the best b'day cake in the world . . . don't you think, Monkey?'

I said, 'Yeah, it really is. It must have cost a fortune.' (Thanks, Uncle Ru xx.)

She was so proud + happy she stood up and banged on her juice glass with a spoon and said, 'Hands up who wants a bit of my cake at tea time?'

Everyone's hands went up. They all shouted, 'Me, me, me! And, 'Nice one!' and, 'Happy Birthday, Jo!' and Mousie was all smiley + glowing and looked v pretty.

We were just leaving to go to first lessons when Harry came over to Mousie with something stuffed in his blazer and said, 'Jo! Shut your eyes, open your hands and see what the fat boy has brought you.'

Next thing, she was holding something fluffy + warm and she was so startled she screamed and let go. Baby bunny leapt out of her arms, hopping round and round M'selle who'd just come in. She said, '*Alors! C'est un petite bébé lapin dans le salle a manger!*'

Harry caught it and said, 'No, miss, it's not a lapin, it's a baby rabbit. It's a b'day present for Joanna Townsend.'

M'selle laughed in French and said, '*Bonne anniversaire*, Zho-anna! Put ze leetle rabbit back in ze 'utch wiz his muzzer until break so he can 'ave a leetle sleep, zen you cudd-url 'im as mesh as you like, OK?'

Mousie's gone with Harry to put Fluff the bunny to bed, so am back in the dorm – got PE next and forgot my kit in the excitement. Am enjoying Mousie's birthday even more than my own!

Kesi always told me, 'It's better to give than receive.' Didn't get what she was banging on about at the time. Thought it was because I kept asking for stuff. But having stuff doesn't make me happy any more. Making Mousie happy does. Better to give. I get it now, Kesi.

Dear Diary,

Aghhh – am so stupid, stupid, stupid! Asked Mousie to come and help me and JT in garden after tea and she said later, after she's written to thank her parents for the wonderful cake + card + book they sent for her b'day. Nooooooooo!

Why did I *not* realise that Mousie was bound to write a thank you letter to her M & D when I made her grand b'day plan?

What if they write back and say they never sent anything? What if Mousie finds out I sent it, not them? She'll guess it was me + hate me + never forgive me and be all lonely again. Don't know what to do. Can't fess up to Mousie and burst her bubble. Wish I could ask someone – Rebekah maybe? But what if I fess to her and she tells me to fess to Mousie and then Mousie's M & D don't reply? If they don't, I might get away with it and Mousie will never know + still feel the love.

But I won't get away with it, will I?

SUNDAY

Dear Diary,

Couldn't write yesterday. Feel sick, I'm so worried Mousie will get a letter from her M & D soon. Dreading school meeting this eve. What have I done!?

MONDAY

Dear Diary,

The worst has happened. Mousie's gone missing. She actually got a letter from her mum today saying she didn't send the cake + book + card and didn't know why she was being thanked. Mousie didn't understand and asked me who could have sent the cake etc.? I thought she'd guess it was me but she trusts me too much. Couldn't tell her. Feel like I've betrayed her. I said, 'Forget it, let's go and see Fluff.'

But she said, 'I want to be on my own. I'm going for a walk.'

That was hours ago. Thought she'd be back by break but she wasn't. Covered for her in lessons and told the teachers Mousie was in bed with bad headache but what if she's had an accident? Will never forgive myself.

Dear Diary,

Lunchtime. Couldn't eat even though it was chocolate krispies for pudding. I'm sick with worry. Still no sign of Mousie. This is why we should be allowed mobile phones in case of emergencies. Fed Fluff for her. Harry hasn't seen Mousie either though. Nor has JT.

Dear Diary,

It's almost tea time – still no Mousie. I've looked everywhere. So scared for her. She's out there somewhere in a storm. It's chucking it down with rain and thundering. What if she gets struck by lightning? She hasn't even got her coat. She'll be soaked. Feel so guilty. Was just trying to do a lovely thing, and now look what's happened. I don't care what happens to me, if she's not home in the next half hour I will have to tell Miss Beauty and Miss Beast that Mousie's gone AWOL. What if the police get involved?

Dear Diary,

Oh dear. Mousie just came back in a terrible state. Found her creeping through the garden door shivering, teeth chattering. Rain was dripping off her. Tried to hurry her upstairs to the dorm to help her out of her wet things but we bumped into Matron. She took one look at Mousie and rushed her to the sick bay. I kept asking Mousie if she was OK but she wouldn't speak so Matron sent me away.

Am in the common room now. Was going to practise scales in the hall but can't concentrate so am planning v important letter instead. Excuse all the crossings-out. It's a really hard thing to write but it has to be done. I found Mousie's address book in her red handbag so I know where to send it. Will copy it out neatly and post it before dinner. Not that I can face any dinner and it's fish and chips. Read what I've put. Do you think it's OK? I'm not sure.

Letter to Mousie's Mum:

Dear Mrs Townsend,

I am writing to ask you a big favour. I am Elizabeth Allen and ~~Mousie~~ Joanna is my best friend but I've done something ~~which you have ruined~~ really stupid.

Sorry to say this next bit but ~~you're a lousy mother~~ Joanna really loves you but thinks you ~~hate her guts~~ don't love her because you ~~can't be bothered~~ hardly ever write or visit and she thought you were going to forget her birthday.

Well, I got £50 from my ~~dodgy~~ uncle and had a good idea. At least I thought it was but it wasn't. I ordered a ~~stonking great~~ big birthday cake that **cost me a fortune** and bought a book and a card and pretended they were from you and Mr Townsend so the others wouldn't ~~call her a loser/think she's an orphan~~ tease her. Kids can be really mean to each other as I'm sure you can remember, ~~even though you are old~~ from the olden days.

It made her so happy but like ~~a twit~~ a fool I forgot she'd write and thank you. When you wrote back and said you hadn't sent them, she took it so badly she stormed off ~~in a storm~~ and now she's ~~dying~~ really ill and she's my best friend and I'm scared for her.

It's all ~~your~~ my fault ~~so don't even think of being angry with me~~ and I don't blame you if you're really angry with me. Everybody always is but I was only trying to make ~~Mousie~~ Joanna happy, I promise.

What I'm writing for is to ask if you would please come and see her and at least ~~buy her a bra/puppy/ shoes that aren't from the pound shop~~ make a big fuss of her, because if you did, I think she would be so happy she'd get better. I am so sorry. ~~I will never forgive you if you don't come~~. Please forgive me.

Yours truly,

Elizabeth Allen

PS: I really am sorry.

Dear Diary,

Just got back from the dining hall. Thought Mousie might have made a miraculous recovery and be there but Carthorse said, 'Haven't you heard? She's still in the sick bay with a really high temperature.'

She could see I was worried and said, 'Cheer up. She'll probs be as right as rain tomorrow.' But it was the rain that made her ill.

And my stupid plan. Want to go and visit Mousie. I saved her some grapes from dinner but I've got to go to that stupid meeting now. Shauna said I'd better not be late or else.

Dear Diary,

Went to the school meeting. Shauna grassed me up about spending Uncle Ru's £50 + not putting it in the box and lying about spending it on Eccles cakes.

Everyone made such a fuss, the head almost

flew off Windy's hammer. Rebekah made me stand up and tell her what I spent the money on so she could at least judge if I'd spent it well or not.

How could I? I said I truly forgot about putting money in the box, and then it was too late. But I couldn't say what I'd bought with it – it's a secret and someone will be really hurt if I tell everyone.

Rebekah said, 'Do you think *we'd* have let you spend the money on what you bought?' and I got upset and said I don't know but that I didn't spend it on myself. She asked if I told anyone else about the secret and I said yes, in a letter to a grown-up but she hasn't replied yet cos I only just posted it. But I know this person will be mad at me.

Rebekah had a little goss with Windy because Miss Beast and Miss Beauty weren't there to give their opinions. Seems they were busy having their own meeting about Mousie because they're so worried.

Thought the jury were going to ask for me to be expelled. But hats off to Rebekah, she decided they shouldn't do anything till I get a reply from my letter because whatever I've done, she could see I'm already punishing myself for it because I was in a right state.

Promised I'll tell her as soon as the person I sent the letter to replies. I even refused to accept my £10 pocket money to show how sorry I am ☹.

Windy said that showed good character and carried on with other business, i.e. Poppy Timms asking for extra money to buy a light bulb because a tin opener flew out of her hand and smashed hers.

Off to the sick bay to visit Mousie now.

Tuesday

Dear Diary,

Matron wouldn't let me see Mousie last night. She's got worse and the doctor said no visitors. Asked if I can at least bring her some flowers later and Matron said she'll give them to her.

I went to the garden at lunchtime to ask JT if I could have some tulips. He said I could pick some of his best pink ones. He was saving them to give to his mum when she comes at half-term but he said Mousie can have them because he knows how much she means to me. Oh, I hope she's going to be OK. I couldn't bear it if anything happened to her. Going to really miss her when I leave. JT said, 'Don't worry, Lizzy. Mousie will be OK, I promise.'

Love it when JT calls me Lizzy. He started off by calling me Busy Lizzy, like the flower. Then just Lizzy. I know what you're thinking, Diary, but shut your little faux-ostrich face. Things change. Get over it.

Taking Mousie's flowers to sick bay now.

Dear Diary,

Am in a state of total shock. Got pulled out of maths and summoned to headmistresses' office just before break.

Agghhhh! Mousie's mum got my letter and has come to see her!

She's in the sick bay right now. She showed Miss Beauty & Miss Beast my letter. I thought they'd go ape at me but they said now they know why I spent Uncle Ru's money on Mousie, they reckon I only broke the rules because I have a good heart and they'll explain everything to Rebekah and Windy.

Mousie's mum wants to see me. I asked Miss Beast if I really had to go and see her. I'm pooping

myself at the thought and she said, 'Yes, dear. Best to get it over with. Chin up, chop, chop!'

Dear Diary,

Yay! Did my happy dance all the way back from the sick bay.

Miss Ranger saw me and thought I'd gone mad. Have met Mousie's mum. She was so lovely. She said she's not cross about my letter AT ALL and is REALLY GLAD I sent it as she had no idea Mousie felt so unloved.

She said she's totally ashamed and deeply sorry for making Mousie feel like that – there is a reason why she hasn't been a good mum but she said Mousie would tell me about it when she feels better because it is v upsetting + personal.

She had a little cry and hugged me + thanked me for being Mousie's friend. Then she hugged Mousie, said she loves her and will always be there for her from now on. I hugged Mousie, who said she's really missed me, then we had a group hug. Matron gave us a big fat box of tissues to dry our eyes while she took Mousie's temperature . . . and it was *normal*!

Mousie is sooo much better! She said she was starving and asked her mum to stay and have tea with us in the dining hall to show her how much she can eat and that she actually has a mum and Mrs Townsend said YES! And Matron said Mousie can get up as long as she doesn't over-do it.

Mrs Townsend said, 'Don't worry, I'll take great care of her, I promise.' Hearing that was like music to Mousie's little felty ears. I'm so happy for her I could burst.

Wednesday

Dear Diary,

Can't believe the change in Mousie. She's like a different person – still my Mousie but like she's eaten a family bag of smiley faces and morphed into one.

We had a long heart to heart last night. Makes me cry when I think about it. Seems Mousie had a twin bro called Bobby. He died when she was two, so she doesn't remember him and her mum never talks about him because his death broke her heart.

Mrs Townsend could not stop grieving so Mousie's dad looked after her alone, but he also had to look after his sad wife, so Mousie didn't get much of a look in.

Mousie said she stopped asking for attention after a while because her dad was so busy working

+ her mum was falling apart so they sent Mousie to Whyteleafe because they couldn't cope, and thought she'd have a better time there.

In her letters home, Mousie always pretended she was happy and had loads of friends because she didn't want to worry them, so they thought everything was hunky-dory.

I said, even so, they could have remembered your b'day. Mousie said she'd asked her mum about that and her M cried and said she never forgot her, it was just that Mousie's b'day is always a sad day for her because it would have been Bobby's birthday too and he isn't here any more.

Going to ask JT if we can plant a little tree for Bobby in the school garden for Mousie to remember him by. I know he'll say yes, because he's the brother I never had. Only he's *not* my brother – phew – because the way I feel about him, that would just be weird + wrong.

Will ask the jury for tree money at the next

meeting. It's the last one before half-term but hopefully I'll get to help JT plant it before I leave. Mousie keeps begging me not to go. Tempted to stay but I have to stick to my guns. Guinea pigs don't live for ever.

Dear Diary,

Rebekah asked me to go to her study 'for a chat' at break.

Nice room! You get your own study if you're Head Girl/Boy. Would love my own study. Windy came in eating a Twix and said, 'Wotcha. How's Elizabeth the Worst?' but he only said it as a joke.

I like him lots now because he said when Miss Beast & Miss Beauty told them what I'd done with Uncle Ru's money, he and Rebekah totally got why I couldn't tell them at the last meeting.

I said I was just trying to protect Mousie. Windy reckons I did the right thing, just in the wrong way and if I'd been at Whyteleafe longer I'd have known I can trust them to help if I have a problem. They'd have let me spend the money on Mousie without getting into trouble if only I'd asked.

I was worried they'd have to bring it up at next meeting and it will be all over the school, but they said they won't. They are satisfied with my explanation, the jury doesn't need to know and 'the matter is closed'. Which is really good of them.

I said, 'Thanks! That's a relief because now Mousie can hold her head up high. Everyone will still think the b'day cake + card + book came from her M & D and next year I won't have to pretend who the presents are from because they'll give her *loads* because they *do* love her, they really do, Windy. I mean Will.'

He laughed and said, 'Next year? So you *are* staying with us? That's good. You'd make a great monitor in a term or two.'

I thought he was taking the micky . . . Me? A MONITOR?!

But he said, 'Yeah, why not?'

I'd LOVE to be a monitor! M & D and Kesi would be so proud of me. I'd be good + fair + helpful + kind but in a firm way – like him and Rebekah. I just need a bit more practice.

'Stay then,' said Rebekah. I told her I'd really like to but can't because I've made up my mind and only losers change their minds.

'Really?' said Windy. 'Where did you get that nutty idea from? We've changed our minds about you – are you calling us losers?'

He said, 'If you're happy here but insist on going home just to prove a point, who's the real loser?' He gave me the other half of his Twix and said to chew it over.

Should I stay or should I go? Got four days to make up my mind.

THURSDAY

Dear Diary,

Only three days left to make up my mind. Still think it would be really wussy to stay after everything I've said though. Embarrassing.

I'm going to really miss Mousie, but she'll be OK, won't she? Carthorse, Ellie and Hamster are really friendly to her now. And I know Mousie's mum will write to her and visit, so I'm not worried about her being sad and lonely any more.

Just me then.

FRIDAY

Dear Diary,

Mousie is blackmailing me. She said if I stay, Harry will give me TWO baby rabbits and they can be friends with Fluff. Everyone needs a friend, she said. Even bunnies.

Even Ricardo Marconi is being spookily nice to me. After we'd practised our duet, Mr Lewis asked me to play my sea piece to Ricardo who was seriously impressed. He told Mr Lewis I should perform it at the end of term concert which is a massive compliment coming from Mr Italy.

Mr Lewis said he's already asked me but I said no, because I am leaving and Ricardo slapped his own forehead and said, '*Why?* You like it here! Whadda you, a chooch? You're a-wasting my time. Ciao, *bimba!*'

And he swanned out! Mr Lewis rolled his eyes and said Ricardo is just upset because he'll have to play the duet with Harry now. He said I'm not to worry. It isn't my problem and I must do what I feel is right.

BUT I DON'T KNOW ANY MORE!

SATURDAY

Dear Diary,

Sitting on the swing at the back of school field. Just had huge row with JT. It was going so well. He said he loves me – helping him in the garden that is – because I know what I'm doing and everyone else only does a bit when they feel like it.

He said he really wants to keep it up because we've got it together now – the garden – but nobody else helps when the seedlings need pricking out or with the weeding.

I said, '*Nobody?* Aren't I somebody?'

He went red and said, 'Yes! But what do you care? If you really love . . . gardening, you wouldn't leave me . . . to do the manuring I mean – when you leave at half-term.'

I said, 'John, I do love y— . . . our garden but I *have* to leave because I've told everyone I'm going and I'll look pathetic if I don't.'

'What about Bobby's tree?' he said.

I yelled, 'Don't say that! That's below the belt! You *know* I want to be with you . . . when you plant it. But a girl has to do what a girl has to do!'

He threw his hoe down and said, 'I give up. Bye then,' and shut himself in the greenhouse.

I HATE him! But I need him like roses need rain and all that manure.

SUNDAY

Dear Diary,

Been awake all night. Have made up my mind about what I'm going to say at the meeting tomorrow. I haven't told Mousie yet. There's no going back. She'll miss the meeting as she has to go to the chiropodist to have a verruca removed. Eughh.

M☹NDAY

Dear Diary,

It's been a funny old day. Don't know whether to laugh or cry. I couldn't finish my dinner even though we had spotted dick. My stomach's in bits. Been to the toilet three times already. Have left my lucky hippo under Mousie's pillow. Going to meeting now.

Dear Diary,

I told you there was no going back, didn't I? And that's because . . . drum roll . . .

I am NOT leaving at half-term.

I AM STAYING AT WHYTELEAFE!

Because it's all RIGHTELEAFE!

When I told Windy + Rebekah this at the meeting they said they ADMIRE me for having the strength of personality to change my mind and said although I had a bad start, I am the sort of person they want at this school and they hope I'll stay here for years.

The jury started clapping – even Humphrey, possibly because I gave him my last Rolo in geography. Harry is so pleased I'm staying he whacked me on the back so hard I swallowed my gum.

Then the best thing happened. JT smiled at me and he WINKED.

He *WINKED*! That must mean he loves me, doesn't it? I was worried it might just be a blink but Carthorse nudged me and said, 'How come JT just winked at you?'

I said, 'Maybe he's got something in his eye.'

But he hasn't got something in his eye, he's got someone.

And she is feeling G☺☺D!

Dear Diary,

Just ran and found Mousie. She's fed up because her foot hurts after her verruca op and she can't go swimming till after half-term.

I said, 'Shame, you like swimming, don't you, Mousie?'

But she pulled a face and said, 'I'm glad I can't go swimming. I won't have anyone to hold my towel up in the changing room because you will have left and I hate people seeing my boobies.'

I grabbed her by the shoulders and said, 'Mousie. Look at me. I promise no one will see your boobies.'

And she said, 'Well, I'm not having Carthorse hold my towel because she peeks.'

And I said, 'Carthorse will not hold your towel, I will.'

She didn't get it for a sec. Then she flung her arms round me and hopped up and down on one foot (couldn't jump properly because of her verruca op) and said, 'Woo-hoo! The lucky hippo worked. It *worked*! You're *staying*, aren't you, Monkey? Say you are!'

I said, 'Yes! Yes!'

And she said, 'Is it because of me?'

And you know what? It *is* because of Mousie because she brings out the best in me and now I'm not Elizabeth the Worst. I'm Elizabeth the Best. Well, maybe not the best. But a whole lot better than I was.

Which means everyone likes me and I've got a best friend for the first time ever *and* baby rabbits. And JT winked at me.

When M & D come and see me at half-term they will not BELIEVE what a changed person I am and beg me to come home for good.

But I won't! If M & D make me leave, I shall be as BAD as I can be until they send me back here.

I LOVE Whyteleafe. It's the best school in the world and if anyone says it isn't, they'll have *me* to deal with.

FRIDAY

Dear Diary,

Sorry I haven't written for few days. Having too much fun. Mum's come to pick me up today and Mousie's mum has come to fetch her. Our mums are carrying on like BFs and swapping notes on where to get Botox or something and they only just met in the car park! They'll be going to Zumba together in matching leotards next.

Oh please don't let them wear leotards.

Miss Beauty & Miss Beast gave me a glowing report and Mum is so proud of me, she's treating me to a cream tea in the village. Mrs Townsend and Mousie will be joining us for scones and jam etc. as soon as Mousie has been fitted with a bra.

Afterwards, me and Mousie are going home to be with our families for the half-term hols. We're gonna keep in touch every day though.

Got my mobile back but weirdly I haven't missed it. Daddy even offered me an upgrade but I said, 'No, thanks. Anyway, you'll need the money to pay for my school fees now I'm staying at Whyteleafe.'

Almost forgot. Mum's so chuffed I'm going to play 'Opus 55' at the end of term concert that she's invited my old piano tutor to see how well I've turned out. Hope her fingers have mended so she can clap. So glad I've finally made M & D proud. Kesi will hardly recognise me when she comes to stay with us at Christmas.

Can't wait to see Ross, Sausage & Beans. Missed them soooo much. *Neighhhh . . . wheep-wheep-wheep!*

Never thought I'd say it, but I'm really going to miss Whyteleafe in the hols – the girls in my dorm, Harry Dunn, Mr Lewis and all.

And JT of course. How could I *ever* forget JT?

Fourteen days seems like such a loooooong time to be away.

Can't wait to come back! ☺☺☺☺☺☺
Yours truly,
Elizabeth Allen
PS: Thanks for listening xxx

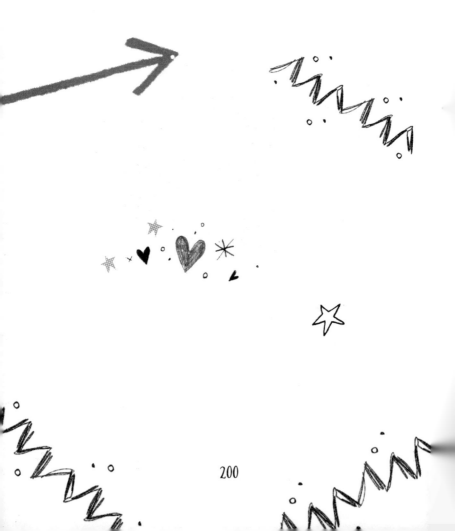